Edgar Wallace was born illegitima
adopted by George Freeman, a port
eleven, Wallace sold newspapers at
school took a job with a printer. He enlisted in the Royal West Kent
Regiment, later transferring to the Medical Staff Corps and was sent
to South Africa. In 1898 he published a collection of poems called
The Mission that Failed, left the army and became a correspondent
for Reuters.

Wallace became the South African war correspondent for *The
Daily Mail*. His articles were later published as *Unofficial Dispatches* and
his outspokenness infuriated Kitchener, who banned him as a war
correspondent until the First World War. He edited the *Rand Daily
Mail*, but gambled disastrously on the South African Stock Market,
returning to England to report on crimes and hanging trials. He
became editor of *The Evening News*, then in 1905 founded the Tallis
Press, publishing *Smith*, a collection of soldier stories, and *Four Just
Men*. At various times he worked on *The Standard*, *The Star*, *The Week-
End Racing Supplement* and *The Story Journal*.

In 1917 he became a Special Constable at Lincoln's Inn and also
a special interrogator for the War Office. His first marriage to Ivy
Caldecott, daughter of a missionary, had ended in divorce and he
married his much younger secretary, Violet King.

The Daily Mail sent Wallace to investigate atrocities in the Belgian
Congo, a trip that provided material for his *Sanders of the River* books.
In 1923 he became Chairman of the Press Club and in 1931 stood as
a Liberal candidate at Blackpool. On being offered a scriptwriting
contract at RKO, Wallace went to Hollywood. He died in 1932, on
his way to work on the screenplay for *King Kong*.

The Three
Oak Mystery

HOUSE OF
STRATUS

Copyright by Edgar Wallace

All rights reserved. No part of this publication may be reproduced, stored in a retrieval system, or transmitted, in any form, or by any means (electronic, mechanical, photocopying, recording, or otherwise), without the prior permission of the publisher. Any person who does any unauthorised act in relation to this publication may be liable to criminal prosecution and civil claims for damages.

The right of Edgar Wallace to be identified as the author of this work has been asserted in accordance with sections 77 and 78 of the Copyright, Designs and Patents Act 1988.

This edition published in 2001 by House of Stratus, an imprint of Stratus Holdings plc, 24c Old Burlington Street, London, W1X 1RL, UK.

www.houseofstratus.com

Typeset, printed and bound by House of Stratus.

A catalogue record for this book is available from the British Library.

ISBN 1-84232-709-7

This book is sold subject to the condition that it shall not be lent, resold, hired out, or otherwise circulated without the publisher's express prior consent in any form of binding, or cover, other than the original as herein published and without a similar condition being imposed on any subsequent purchaser, or bona fide possessor.

This is a fictional work and all characters are drawn from the author's imagination. Any resemblance or similarities to persons either living or dead are entirely coincidental.

CONTENTS

INTRODUCING SOCRATES SMITH

"Murder is neither an art nor a science, it is an accident," said Socrates Smith, and Lex Smith, his younger brother, his most devoted admirer and his dearest trial, grinned sardonically.

A greater contrast between the two men it would be difficult to imagine. "Soc" Smith was nearing fifty and was a lean, tall, stooping man with a lined face – it seemed to be carved by careless hands from a block of seasoned teak. A tiny iron grey moustache lay above a firm mouth, set tight and straight.

Lex was twenty-five years his junior, and two inches shorter. But so straight was his back that most people thought the brothers were of the same height, and if they had had to say offhand which was the taller, would, with little hesitation, have named the good-looking boy.

"Lordy, Uncle Soc," said Lex Smith solemnly, "how you do aphorise!"

"If you call that an aphorism you're a goop," said Soc. "Pass the marmalade."

They were sitting at breakfast in the big dining-room overlooking Regent's Park. The brothers occupied the first and second floors of one of those big houses in the outer circle of Regent's Park. The house was the property of Socrates Smith and had been acquired by him when he was in his thirties.

In those days he had vague ideas of matrimonial responsibility. But though he had secured the house he had never had time to fall in love, and expended what Lex described as his "maternal instincts" in the care of his baby brother.

Life had been too full for Socrates Smith to allow room for the gentle distractions of courtship, and there were times when he blessed the Tollemarsh murder which had occupied his every thought at a period when his aunt, his one relative in the world save Lex, had planned an alliance, and had made the most elaborate preparations for hurrying him into the blessed state. For the lady chosen had since been three times through the Divorce Court and had a London reputation.

Soc had taken up the study of crime as a regular member of the constabulary. Probably there never was before or since a policeman who walked his beat by day and night and spent his leisure hours in one of London's most exclusive clubs.

He had an income of six thousand a year, but police work had been his passion, and as there was no other way, in those days, of securing admission to the books of the Criminal Investigation Department but through service in the uniformed branch, he had served his hard apprenticeship as a "cop."

For four years he had been alternately office man and executive officer, with the rank of Sergeant – an amazingly rapid promotion, and then he had resigned from the force and had devoted himself to the examination of foreign police methods and the even more fascinating study of anthropology.

Scotland Yard is a very jealous and a very loyal institution. It looks askance at the outsider and turns a freezing stare upon the enthusiastic amateur, but Soc had left the Yard with the good wishes of the administration and had contributed to the sum of official knowledge.

When the fingerprint system was installed, he was called in and worked with an official status, and it was usual to consult him in cases where especial difficulties confronted the patient investigators. So that Socrates knew something of fame. He was an acknowledged authority upon fingerprints and bloodstains, and was the first man to standardize the spectrum and guaiacum tests for the discovery of blood upon clothing.

"What train are we catching?" asked Lexington.

"Two o'clock from Waterloo," said his brother, rolling his serviette.

"Am I going to be bored?" demanded Lex.

"Yes," replied the other, with a twinkle in his eye, "but it will be good for your soul. Boredom is the only discipline which youth cannot reject."

Lex laughed.

"You're full of wise sayings this morning," he said. "Prophetically were you named Socrates!"

Socrates Smith had long since forgiven his parents for his eccentric name. His father had been a wealthy iron-founder with a taste for the classics, and it had only been the strenuous opposition of their mother which had prevented Lex from being named "Aristophanes."

"If a child's birth name is Smith, my dear," Smith senior said with truth, "he should have something striking and distinguishing before it."

They had compromised on "Lexington," for it was in Lexington Lodge, Regent's Park, that the boy had been born.

"I'm full of wise sayings, am I?" repeated Soc Smith, showing his small white teeth in a smile, "well, here's another. Propinquity is more dangerous than beauty."

Lex stared at him.

"Meaning, how?" he asked.

"Mandle's daughter is reputedly lovely, and you're going to spend three days in the same house – *verbum sapient*."

"Bosh!" said the younger man inelegantly, "I don't fall in love with every girl I meet."

"You haven't met many," was the answer.

Later in the morning Lex interrupted his packing to stroll into his brother's room. At that moment Socrates was cursing with great calmness the inadequacy of his one battered suitcase which refused to accommodate all the personal belongings he wished to take with him on his visit.

"Why not shoot out the impedimenta of your noxious craft?" asked Lex, pointing to a small brown box which he knew contained his brother's microscope, "you aren't likely to light upon a murder at Hindhead."

"You never know," replied Socrates hopefully. "If I didn't take it something would happen – packing it ensures a quiet and peaceable weekend."

"What sort of a fellow is Mandle?" demanded the youth, remembering why he had come into the room.

"He was a very good officer and a brilliant detective," said Socrates. "He's not an easy man to get on with by any means, but when he left the police at the height of his career, the force lost a good man. He and Stone left together. Stone lives within – well, within a stone's throw."

He chuckled.

"A feeble jest," said his critical brother. "Stone was an inspector of the CID also?"

"Sergeant," said Socrates; "they were bosom friends, and when Mandle began speculating on the Stock Exchange, Stone followed him and they made pots of money. Mandle was quite frank about it. He saw the Chief Commissioner and told him that he couldn't keep his mind on two things, and do both properly, and so he had decided to chuck the police.

"He was a disappointed man, too; he had set his heart upon capturing Deveroux, the man who robbed the Lyons Bank, and got away to South America, and the fellow slipped through his fingers. That and one or two other happenings brought an unofficial reprimand from the chief. Still, the old man was quite upset when Mandle got out.

"Stone was a clever chap, too, so the Yard lost two really good men at a time when they couldn't spare one."

"Three, you old fossil," said Lex, slapping his brother on the back. "You got out about the same time."

Oh yes," said the indifferent Socrates, "but I didn't count."

JOHN MANDLE'S STEPDAUGHTER

"The Woodlands," John Mandle's home, was delightfully sited on the slope of a hill. Four acres of pine and gorseland surrounded it, and the house itself was invisible from the road.

It stood a mile away from Hindhead, and from its sloping lawns John Mandle could command a view over miles of pleasant country.

He sat in his drawing-room, a thick rug over his knees, gazing gloomily through the French windows at the pleasant countryside. A grim grey man with a strong face, and a heavy jaw, he communicated some of his own gloom to his surroundings.

A girl who came in with his letters stood meekly by whilst he glanced through them.

"No wire from Smith," he growled.

"No, father," said the girl quietly.

Socrates Smith had not exaggerated when he described her as lovely. Ordinarily, loveliness is a little inhuman, but this girl radiated humanity. In the presence of her stepfather she was chilled, repressed, and as near to being colourless as it was possible for her to be. She feared the man – that was apparent; hated him a little, probably, remembering the hardness of her dead mother's lot and the tyranny which she had inherited.

Mandle had no children of his own and never seemed to feel the need for them. His attitude to the girl was that of a master to a superior servant, and in all the days of their acquaintance he had never once shown her the least tenderness or regard.

His caprice had taken her from a good boarding school and the pleasant associations of children of her own class and age, and had brought her to the strained atmosphere of "The Woodlands," to the society of a nerve-racked wife and a glowering unreasonable man, who would go for days without speaking a word. She felt that he had cheated her – cheated her of the happiness which her school had brought to her, cheated her of the means by which she could have secured a livelihood and independence, cheated her of all of her faith in men and much of her faith in God.

"Are the two rooms ready?" he barked.

"Yes, father," she replied.

"You have got to do your best to make them comfortable," he ordered. "Socrates Smith is an old friend of mine – I haven't met his brother."

A faint smile played about the corner of the girl's mouth.

"It's a curious name he has," she said.

"If it's good enough for him, it's good enough for you," said John Mandle.

The girl was silent.

"I haven't seen Socrates for ten years," John Mandle went on, and she felt that he was really thinking aloud, for he would not trouble to take the girl into his confidence. "Ten years! A clever fellow – a wonderful fellow!"

She made another attempt to enter into conversation.

"He is a great detective, isn't he?" she asked, and expected to be snapped up, but to her surprise he nodded.

"The greatest and the cleverest in the world – at any rate, in England," he said, "and from what I hear his brother is likely to follow in his footsteps."

"Is the brother young?"

John Mandle looked up under his shaggy brows and eyed her coldly.

"He is twenty-five," he said. "Now understand once and for all that I'll have no philandering, Molly."

Molly's lovely face flushed red and her round chin rose with a jerk.

"I am not in the habit of philandering with your guests," she said, her voice trembling with anger. "Why do you say such beastly things to me?"

"That will do," he said, with a jerk of his head.

"It will do for you, but not for me," said the girl hotly. "I have endured your tyranny ever since poor mother's death, and I have come to the end of my patience. You have made this beautiful place a living hell for me, and I will endure it no longer."

"If you don't like it, you can get out," he said, without turning his head.

"That is precisely what I intend doing," she replied more quietly. "I will wait till your guests have gone, and then I will go to London and earn my own living."

"And a nice job you'll make of it," he sneered. "What can you do?"

"Thanks to you I can do nothing," she said. "If you had left me at school I should at least have had an education which would have fitted me for a teacher."

"A teacher," he laughed harshly. "What rubbish you talk, Molly. You understand that if you leave me in the lurch you get not a penny of my money when I die."

"I don't want your money – I have never wanted your money," she cried passionately. "My mother left me a few trinkets – "

"Which I bought her," growled the other. "She had no right to leave my property to you."

"At any rate I haven't seen much of them," replied the girl.

She was turning to leave the room when he called her back.

"Molly," he said, in a softer tone than she had ever heard him use, so unexpectedly gentle that she stopped, "you've got to make allowances for me – I'm a very sick man."

She softened at this.

"I'm sorry, father," she replied. "I ought to have remembered that – are your knees very bad?"

"So bad that I can't stand," he growled. "It is damned annoying this rheumatism coming on when I've invited my old friend down to see me. This means that I shall be in bed for a week. Send the men here and tell them to bring the wheeled chair; I want to go into my study to work."

With the assistance of the gardener and his valet, John Mandle was trundled into a big airy room which he had built at the side of the house on the ground floor level, a room which served as study and bedroom whenever he felt disinclined to mount the stairs to his own room, for he was subject to these rheumatic attacks.

The girl, after seeing him comfortably placed at his table, went about her household duties.

Mandle's chair was on the lawn before the house when Socrates Smith and his brother drove up that afternoon.

"Hullo," said Soc, surprised, "what's the matter with you, John?"

"This infernal rheumatism," snarled the other. "I'm glad to see you, Socrates; you look just about the same."

"This is my brother," said Socrates, and the younger man shook hands.

They did not see the girl until Lexington had wheeled the chair into the drawing-room for tea, and the sight of her took the young man's breath away.

"She's wonderful, Socrates," he said enthusiastically when they were alone after the meal. "She's divine! Did you ever see such eyes, and the skin — my heavens! it's as pure and as speckless as a rose-leaf; and did you notice her wonderful carriage – "

"Oh, Lex, you make me tired," said Socrates wearily, "to think that I should have brought you down here and undone the work of years. After having kept you sheltered from the wiles of females – "

"Oh, shut up," said Lexington. "You know jolly well she's beautiful."

"She isn't bad," admitted the cautious Socrates; "to me she's just a girl."

"You're a heathen and a Philistine," snapped his brother.

"I can't be both," said the philosophical Soc. "What I did notice – " He stopped, out of loyalty to his friend.

"What was that?" asked Lexington expectantly. "The way he treated her?"

8

Socrates nodded.

"He's a bully," said Lex, emphatically; "and a man who can be so lost to a sense of decency that he talks to a girl like that, as if she were a dog, is beyond my understanding. Did you hear him snarl at her about the sugar?"

"I think he hates her," said Socrates, thoughtfully, "and I'm pretty certain that she hates him. It is an interesting household, because John Mandle is scared."

"Scared?"

Soc Smith nodded, for he had seen the fear of death in John Mandle's eyes.

THE FEAR OF JOHN MANDLE

"Scared of what?" Lexington's eyebrows rose.

"I'd like to know," repeated Socrates quietly. "Did you see the wire alarm near the gate? Did you notice the study door has an electrical lock? You wouldn't, of course, because you're a cub at the game. Did you see the revolver at his hand, both in his bedroom and in his study, and the triple mirror over his writing-table, so that he can look up and see all that is happening behind him and on either side? He is scared – scared to death, I tell you. He has the fear of fears in his eyes!"

Lexington could only look at his brother open-mouthed.

"That is partly the reason he is such a grump, so you'll have to make allowances for him – And here is Bob Stone," he said suddenly, and walked across the lawn to meet the man who was striding up the drive. A bluff, broad-shouldered man with a good-humoured face, the newcomer bellowed his greeting to his old comrade in a voice that could be heard for miles.

"Soc, you're skinnier than ever," he shouted. "By gad, you are just bones held together by parchment! Don't you ever eat?"

Socrates Smith grinned as he took the other's huge paw in his and shook it.

"You're as noisy as ever, Bob," he said, and looked round for John Mandle.

"He is groaning in the hands of a masseur," said Lexington.

"This is your brother – I don't remember him. A good looker, Socrates, a real good looker. Don't you think so, Miss Templeton?"

The girl's eyes danced at the evidence of Lexington's embarrassment.

"I am no judge of male beauty," she said demurely. "I see nobody but father and you."

Bob Stone roared at the malicious thrust and slapped his knee, an operation which reminded him of his friend's misfortune.

"Poor John has a very bad time with his legs," he said, "a shocking bad time. What he wants is a little faith and little more religion in his system."

Socrates looked at him sharply.

"That's a new note in you, Bob," he said.

"What, religion? Yes, I suppose it is, but I'm rather inclined that way lately. It's a pity you can't stay over for our big revival meeting at Godalming. Evans, the Welsh evangelist, is coming down – it will be interesting. I'm going to talk."

"You!" said Socrates in surprise.

Bob Stone nodded. His big face was preternaturally solemn.

"Yes, I'm going to address the meeting. Heaven knows what I'm going to say," he said, "but the words will come into my mouth, and I shan't make a fool of myself. Hullo, John!"

John Mandle was propelling himself toward them on his chair, and nodded glumly to his old comrade.

"A revival meeting, did I hear you say? Your voice is like an angel's whisper, Bob."

Bob chuckled.

"Yes, next week there's a meeting in Godalming which I'm going to address. Why don't you come along, John, and get your rheumatism cured?"

John muttered something uncomplimentary to faith healing in general, and the Welsh evangelist in particular, and Stone seemed to treat his wrath as a huge joke.

It was a pleasant day in early summer and they lingered out of doors till the very last moment.

The girl, in some trepidation, had intruded herself into the circle, had even ventured a few comments, and had been surprised that she had not been rudely interrupted by her boorish stepfather. For his forbearance she had probably to thank Lexington Smith, though she dreaded the caustic comments which would follow as a matter of course when she and the tyrant were alone.

"Doesn't it remind you of a meeting of the 'Three Musketeers', Miss Templeton?" asked Lex, and she smiled.

"Talking over their dirty work of other days, and revelling in the recollection of the poor devils they had sent to penal servitude, to the gallows – " Lex went on.

"Mostly of people we failed to send to penal servitude," interrupted Socrates. "Failures are much more interesting than successes, as food for reminiscence, Lex. You will have plenty to talk about in your old and middle age."

"I thank you for the compliment," said Lexington politely.

"I think your brother is rather wonderful," said the girl, lowering her voice. "What extraordinary eyes he has."

"I'm supposed to have rather good eyes," said the shameless youth, and she bubbled with laughter.

"No, Socrates is really remarkable," he went on more seriously. "He is the soundest all-round man at the game, and he is a constant wonder to me. We were talking about your father – "

"My stepfather," she corrected quietly.

"I beg your pardon – your stepfather." It was rude of him to apologize within the hearing of John Mandle, but Mr Mandle was at that moment engrossed in the recital of an early experience, and did not hear it.

"Soc was telling me that Mr Mandle and Mr Stone were the greatest strategists that ever worked at Scotland Yard. They were people who could work out a plan of campaign to the minutest detail, and it was this quality which brought them their success."

They tarried till the dinner gong sounded, and then went into the house, and the meal was a fairly pleasant one. Bob Stone was the type of man who dominated all conversation; he had a fund of stories which seemed inexhaustible, and even Mandle smiled – sourly, it is true – once or twice in the course of the meal.

Lexington wheeled him into the drawing-room, to the bridge table, but to the youth's delight Stone refused to play.

"That is one of the frivolities which I am giving up," he said.

"You're getting sanctimonious in your old age, Bob," sneered Mandle, but the big man only smiled.

He took his leave about an hour later, and John Mandle discussed this new development in his old-time friend with great frankness and acrimony.

"Anything for a sensation, that's Bob's weakness," he said, as he chewed an unlit cigar. "It's the one bad quality which I've tried to drill out of him. Anything for a sensation! Why – he'd ruin himself to get a little applause."

"Maybe he has genuinely got religion," said Socrates. "Such things have happened."

"Not he," said John Mandle contemptuously.

"Is he married yet?"

For about the third time that evening Mandle smiled – his eyes looked across the room to where the girl was sitting with Lexington.

"No – not married," he said quietly, "though he has ambitions in that direction."

"I see," said Socrates, quietly.

The words carried to Lexington and he gasped.

"Not you," he said in a low voice to the girl, and she nodded.

"And you?"

She shrugged her shoulders.

"I like him; of course, he's a dear, but not in that way; it is hopelessly ridiculous, and I told him so."

"What does your father think?"

She did not reply for a moment.

"I think my father lost all interest when he found that I did not favour the match," she said, a little bitterly. "If he had thought I was going to get any happiness out of it there would have been trouble."

Lex said nothing. The fascination of the girl was on him; and it was not because women were an unusual factor in his life.

The two hours which followed passed like minutes to two of the party, and Lexington was surprised, and a little disgusted, when his brother rose.

"I think I'll go to bed," said Socrates. "The country air has made me sleepy. Are you coming up, Lex?"

Lex hesitated.

"Yes," he said, for he had noted the signal in his brother's eye.

"Coming into my room?" said the elder man when they reached the landing above. "I suppose you know you've made John Mandle as sore as a scalded cat?" he said when he had closed the door.

"I have?" replied Lexington, in surprise.

"Listen," said Socrates, and bent his head.

Their room was situated above the drawing-room, and from below came a murmur of angry voices.

"I was afraid he'd rag her," said Socrates quietly.

"But why?"

"The Lord knows," said Socrates, taking off his coat. "But apparently he hates any attention being paid to the girl, and really, Lex, when you were not, as the novelists say, devouring her with your eyes, you were glued to her side."

"Is that an offence?" asked Lexington sarcastically. "Is it unnatural?"

"Very natural, indeed, Lex," said Socrates smiling. "I don't like John's way of conducting his household. An average man would be proud to have such a daughter, even though she's only his step-daughter; but the man's fear has unbalanced him."

"You stick to that theory?" said Lexington.

Socrates nodded.

"Did you see his valet come in? Well, that fellow has had instructions to make the round of the grounds and fix the wires and contraptions with which Mandle guards his house."

"Did you ask him about it?"

Socrates shook his head.

"It is not wise to ask a man about his fears," he said. "It is a subject on which he never grows very voluble."

They heard the quick step of the girl as she passed their room, and presently the heavy tread of the two servants carrying Mr Mandle to bed.

"Good night, John," Soc called as he passed.

"Good night," with a grunt, he replied.

"Good night, Mr Mandle," said Lexington, but there was no answer.

"You have what is colloquially known as 'the bird,'" said Soc with a chuckle.

It was a beautiful moonlight night and they sat by the open casement window smoking until the household was silent and the last rumble of servants' heavy feet had ceased to shake the ceiling.

They talked in soft tones of people, of the beauty of the country on such a night as this, and Lexington was rising with a yawn when his brother asked: "What house is that?"

He pointed across the valley to a big white house clearly visible in the moonlight.

"It's rum you should ask that, for it's the only house in the neighbourhood I know," said Lexington. "I saw it when I was strolling on the lawn this afternoon, and asked one of the gardeners. It belongs to a Mr Jetheroe, a philanthropist and recluse, and a friend of Molly Templeton's, though I should imagine that her father does not know. She –" He did not finish his sentence.

From one of the big windows of the white house flashed a light. Rather would it be more exact to say, the window lit up with an unearthly glow, which died away instantly.

"What was that?" asked Lexington.

Again the window glowed, and then was dark. And then it lit in a rapid succession of flashes.

"Somebody's signalling; that is the Morse code," said Socrates, and spelt – "C – O – M – E." He could not catch the next, and it was some time before he picked up the thread of the message. "REE OAKS," he read, and interpreted the letters as "THREE OAKS."

"I wonder who the dickens is carrying out this clandestine correspondence," he asked.

"I'll give you three guesses," said Lexington with a smile, as he rose; "but if we said it was a demobilized soldier servant who had taught his lady-love the art and method of signalling, we should probably be near the mark."

"Look!" whispered Socrates, excitedly for him. A slim, almost ghostly, figure was moving stealthily along the edge of the lawn in the shadow of a bush hedge.

Lex looked, and his eyes went round. It was Molly Templeton, and she carried a small bag in her hand.

Presently she disappeared and the two men looked at one another.

"There is no reason why she should not take a midnight stroll," said Socrates, and Lex nodded.

"Good night, Soc, old bird, sleep well," he said as he rose; "and call me in the morning when you go for your threatened stroll. I suppose when you said you were going to get up early and go for a walk, it wasn't swank on your part?"

"You'll know all about it," said Socrates grimly.

THE MAN ON THE TREE

Lexington "knew all about it." A wet sponge was pushed into his face and he sat up in bed blinking and gasping. This awakening had interrupted a dream in which John Mandle and the cloaked figure of Molly creeping across the lawn were inextricably mixed.

"Time to get up, my boy," said Socrates softly. He was already dressed, the window was open, and the land lay shrouded in the morning mist, through which the sun was glowing.

"What time is it?" asked Lexington drowsily, as he reached for his slippers.

"Half-past six, and you've seven miles to walk before you must think of breakfast."

An hour later they let themselves out of the house. It was a late-rising household. John Mandle had warned them as to this. He himself did not put in an appearance until noon, and he had hinted that it was very probable that he would spend the day in bed.

They had to pick their way over almost invisible threads which connected alarm guns, and in one case an ingenious magnesian flare, before they came to the road.

"I'm puzzled about that signal last night," said Socrates, as they swung down the hill side by side. "If you remember, we only saw half of the white house; the rest of it was cut off by the angle of the wall. There it is now," he pointed with his stick. The house looked like a white jewel in the early morning sunlight, for the mist was clearing. Behind, and a little to the right, they saw the red gables of Prince's Place, which was Mr Bob Stone's demesne.

"I don't think I should worry my head about it, Soc," said Lexington cheerfully. "What a horrible old detective you are. You must be looking for mysteries, even in this pleasant place."

He himself was puzzled about the girl, but he hesitated to put his speculations into words.

Their walk brought them nearer to the White House. It was a plain, square building, with huge windows that glistened in the sunlight.

"That fellow likes a lot of light," said Socrates. "Do you notice those windows on the ground floor, and the unusual size of those on the upper?"

"Proceed with your deductions, oh great man," said Lexington. "I will be your Doctor Watson."

"Don't be a fool," growled Socrates, who was rather sensitive on one point. "There's a path here down into the valley. We'll follow that and get a nearer view of the White House."

The path was a narrow one, and they had not been walking for five minutes before Socrates stopped.

"Three Oaks!" he said, and pointed. Just ahead of them were three large oak trees, and the path followed a course which would bring them under their spreading branches.

"That's what it was – Three Oaks."

"There are always Three Oaks in a place like this, just as there's always a One Tree Hill and a Three Bridges," said Lexington. "Speaking for myself, I am not sufficiently romantic to be interested in a lover's tryst. I wonder if Mr Mandle takes this walk – it is delightful."

Soc smiled.

"Poor old John would be glad to be able to walk two yards," he said. "He hasn't left his grounds on his own feet for months."

They had to pass through an avenue of bushes and momentarily lost sight of the trees. The path turned abruptly to the left and brought them to within a dozen feet of the nearest tree. And suddenly Lexington felt his arm gripped.

"Great God!" said Socrates Smith, and pointed. A thick branch from the nearest tree overhung the path and lying flat along that branch, tied there securely with a rope, was a man; his hands hung helplessly down above the path, his face turned toward them, and between his eyes was a purple mark where a bullet had struck him.

Socrates raced to the tree and looked up. There was no room for doubt in his mind.

It was John Mandle, dead – murdered!

THE SHOE AND MR JETHEROE

They stood, as if petrified, looking up at the ghastly object, and Lexington was the first to move. His foot was raised to take an impetuous step forward, when Soc, who had not released his grip of the boy's arm, pulled him back.

"Stay where you are," he said sternly.

"It's Mandle!" whispered Lex, and Soc nodded.

"It's Mandle all right," he said grimly, and dropped his eyes from the bough to the ground beneath. "The earth is a little too hard to leave any impression," he said regretfully. "Go ahead carefully, but don't put your foot down on anything that looks like a print."

Presently he stood under the branch and by reaching up and standing on tiptoe could just touch the dead man's hand.

"Look carefully round, Lex, and see what you can find. I am going up that tree."

With extraordinary agility he scrambled up the gnarled trunk and found it a comparatively easy matter, for it was inclined at an angle. Some other climber had been there, and recently. In several places the bark was torn and there was an impress of a man's nailed boots. It was an easy matter to reach the branch where the murdered man lay, and Lexington, watching his brother, saw that he paid little or no attention to the body, save to take a long scrutiny of its feet. He seemed more interested in the branches above, and peered up in his short-sighted way, a mannerism of his, for the eyesight of Socrates Smith was remarkably good.

Presently he came back and dropped lightly to the ground.

20

"Yes," he said.

"Yes what?" asked Lexington curiously, but Soc offered no explanation.

Evidently he had seen something which he had expected to see.

"Did you find anything?" he asked.

"This," said Lex, and handed him a little brass cylinder.

Soc looked at the cartridge case and nodded.

"A 35 automatic," he said. "I knew that it was a nickel-jacketed bullet by the wound it made. Anything else?"

Lex shook his head.

"It's horrible, isn't it?" he said in a whisper, looking up at that terrible face staring down upon them with its blank eyes.

"Fairly horrible," said his brother quietly, "but remarkably interesting."

Lexington Smith was not sufficiently experienced to take a detached interest in the crime as an artistic performance. To him the limp, inanimate figure was that of his host, a man who had been alive and well, and with whom he had been talking on the previous evening.

What a terrible shock for the girl! He remembered her suddenly.

"How could they have done it?" he asked. "There must have been more than one in this. They must have come into the house while we were sleeping, Soc; that's the horrible thought."

"How many people do you think?" asked Socrates quietly.

"At least three," replied his brother. "They must have taken him out of bed, and yet we heard nothing. Do you think they drugged him?"

"I think lots of things," said his brother evasively. "Now, Lex, just tell me what you think happened."

Lexington was silent for a moment.

"He must have some very bad enemies," he said. "You told me he was afraid and evidently expected some such attack as this. In the night they secured admission to his room, and either drugged him or terrified him into silence, and then carried him out to this lonely spot and murdered him."

Socrates shook his head.

"Why not murder him in the house?" he said. "If they could drug him, why not poison him? Why take the trouble to carry him for nearly a mile in order to have the satisfaction of shooting him at their leisure? No, my son, that theory doesn't work!"

"But they must have carried him," insisted Lexington. "Poor Mandle hadn't the use of his legs. And, Soc! do you remember the flashlight – the signal?"

"I haven't forgotten that," said his brother quietly. "Now, Lex, go back to the house and telephone to the police. I'll stay here."

As luck would have it, Lexington had no need to go back to the house. When he climbed the path and emerged on to the main road the first person he saw was a policeman riding leisurely down the hill on his bicycle. Lexington stopped him and told him what had occurred in a few words.

"Murdered?" said the policeman incredulously. "Mr Mandle?"

He wheeled his bicycle into a clump of bushes.

"Just wait a minute, sir," he said," my inspector will be along here in about three minutes. We ought to tell him, and it will save me telephoning."

The inspector made his appearance in five minutes and stopped his tiny car at his subordinate's signal. The three men made their way back to the scene of the tragedy.

Socrates Smith had disappeared, but they heard him working through the thick bushes to the left of the path. After a while he emerged, carrying in his hand a pair of gum shoes which he put down carefully.

Lexington had revealed the identity of his brother, and the name of Socrates Smith was one to be respected.

"Well, Mr Smith, this is a very bad business," said the officer.

"Pretty bad," said Socrates, glancing keenly up at the body.

"It is bewildering," said the inspector. "Why did they tie him?"

"He's not tied very securely, I think you'll find," said Socrates. "The rope has just been thrown up at the body and has swung round him by its own momentum. It has the appearance of being tightly bound, but the first thing I saw when I went up the tree was that both ends of the rope are loose. He maintains his position on the branch by natural balance. There are no footmarks of any kind."

"The ground is a little too hard," said the inspector, disappointed, and then he brightened. "If they came from or went through the valley they'd have to pass across a bit of soft ground. There's a spring about a hundred yards further on which keeps the path muddy."

"Is that so?" said Socrates quickly. "Then that explains – " he picked up the goloshes and exposed the soles. They were covered with a thin cake of yellow mud which had dried. "I wondered how that came about," he said.

The inspector took up the shoes and examined them.

"They're new," he said unnecessarily and shook his head. "These sort of things are sold by the hundred and unless they were bought at Godalming or some local town it would be difficult to trace the buyer."

Socrates Smith nodded.

"That is mystery number one unravelled," he said. "I couldn't understand why they wanted goloshes."

"There was only one pair, I suppose?"

"Only one pair," said Smith gravely, "because only one person was concerned in this murder."

Lexington looked at his brother and gasped.

"Only one?" he said incredulously. "Do you mean to say that one person could have carried him a mile?"

"I say there was only one person concerned in the murder," said Socrates carelessly.

"There must have been more, Mr Smith." It was the inspector who spoke. "You probably don't know that Mr Mandle was a martyr to rheumatism and hasn't walked for a month. I was only talking to him about the matter two or three days ago."

"I know," interrupted Soc quietly. "My brother and I are guests of his."

"Staying at the house?" asked the officer in surprise, and Soc nodded.

23

"Nevertheless I maintain that there was only one person concerned in this murder," he said, and the inspector drew a long breath.

"Well, he must have been a remarkable one person," he said.

"Now let us have a look at the muddy patch," said Socrates. "I think we shall find impressions of the goloshes, which by the way are number twelves and have been worn by somebody with a bigger foot than a twelve, for the left shoe has burst a little."

They followed the winding path for a few hundred yards and came to a place where it dipped down and crossed a distinctly marshy patch. Here the yellow earth was turned to a dark grey and was moist and plastic.

"Be careful now," warned Socrates, "there are half a dozen footprints here, but most of them are old. Here are our goloshes."

He squatted down and pointed to an impression which had obviously been made by overshoes. The corrugations of the sole were plainly visible, but there was only the mark of one sole. They found the other impression five feet away on the farther side of the wet patch.

"A long-striding gentleman, this," said the inspector, but Socrates shook his head.

"He jumped this patch," he said. "Do you see how deep the toe impression is where he took off and how heavy he came down, on the other side? He was familiar with the lay of the land, for he made no mistake in estimating the width of the jump."

"What is that?" asked Lexington pointing.

Socrates followed the direction of the finger which was extended toward an even muddier area to the right of the path.

"Good Lord!" said Socrates, and squelching through the mud, stooped and picked up a shoe.

It was a lady's shoe, deeply embedded in the heavy clay and near at hand was a small footmark showing the natural form of a foot.

"A woman's shoe: that may be important," said the inspector. "Somebody evidently got into that morass and left her shoe behind her."

Socrates nodded.

"And it also looks as if she was trying to avoid leaving a mark on the path," he said.

It was a small shoe, almost new, and he examined it curiously.

"An American made brogue," he said, and pulled back the tongue.

On the underside the leather was undressed and somebody had written the initials "M T".

"M T" he repeated – "Molly Templeton!"

"Molly Templeton!" repeated Lex. "Good heavens, Soc, she couldn't have been here! She – "

Then in a flash he remembered the dark form that he had seen stealing across the lawn on the previous night.

Molly Templeton! That radiant girl! What could she have been doing there, and why should she have tried to avoid leaving her footmarks in the mud?

He looked bewildered at Socrates and there was a little gleam of laughter in his brother's eyes, an unexpected gleam, because Socrates was a grave man in such crises as this.

"Where does this path lead to?" he asked suddenly.

"To the White House. Mr Jetheroe's house."

Soc nodded.

"Who is Mr Jetheroe?" he asked.

The inspector seemed at some loss to describe Mr Jetheroe in adequate and understandable terms.

"He's a writing gentleman," he said. "I don't know what he is by profession, but I know he writes scientific articles. He is a very quiet, nice man, and a friend of Miss Mandle's."

Evidently the inspector did not know that Molly was the step-daughter, for he went on: "Who is Molly Templeton?"

To Lexington's surprise, his brother replied: "The name of a girl I know. It struck me as a coincidence, that's all. Has Jetheroe lived long in the neighbourhood?"

"About four years," said the inspector. "He came here about two months after the late Mrs Mandle died. He had been abroad, I think."

"Been abroad, eh?" said Socrates thoughtfully.

He walked ahead with Lexington along the path towards Mr Jetheroe's house, leaving the inspector and the policeman to guard the body.

"Naturally Mandle has many enemies," he explained. "He has sent quite a number of promising young gentlemen to penal servitude, and, although one doesn't take a great deal of notice of the threats which criminals utter in their anger at the moment of sentence, yet now and again you do find a convict who nurses a plan for vengeance through the long terms of imprisonment."

"Do you think that this is such a case?" asked Lex.

"It may be," replied Socrates; "it may be. Anyway, I am always suspicious of people who suddenly appear in a neighbourhood after having been 'abroad' for a long time."

Smoke was coming from the chimneys of Jetheroe's house when they passed through the gates and up the gravel drive.

A maid-servant, a little fluttered by the appearance of strangers at this hour, opened the door to them.

"Mr Jetheroe is in his room," she said. "What name shall I say?"

"Just say Smith, and tell him that we've come on rather important business," replied Socrates.

He was ushered into a large and somewhat untidy workroom, and a man sitting at a big oak table covered with an untidy litter of paper, rose and looked at them from under his bushy white eyebrows.

"A remarkable-looking man," thought Socrates, with reason. He stood over six feet in height, and the spareness of his frame gave the illusion of an even greater height.

The face was thin and refined. The hair flowed back over his collar, a white mane.

Lexington was reminded of the portrait of the great musician, Liszt.

"Good morning, gentlemen," said Mr Jetheroe.

His manner was not particularly genial. Indeed, there was in his hard, harsh voice something menacing and, to Lexington's impressionable mind, forbidding.

"What can I do for you?"

"I have come to see you in relation to Mr John Mandle," said Socrates quietly, and he thought he saw the man start.

"Yes, I know Mr John Mandle by sight," said Jetheroe. "Sit down, please. Did he send you?

"Mandle is dead," said Soc quietly.

"Dead!"

Some queer emotion was expressed in the sudden flash of his eyes and the scarcely observable change of countenance.

"Dead! you say?"

"He was murdered last night, within a few hundred yards of this house," said Socrates, and there was a dead silence.

"That is very interesting," said Jetheroe, and his voice was cold and hard. "And, of course, very dreadful. Have you found the murderer?"

"We are seeking for him now," said Smith.

"You are a detective?"

Socrates smiled.

"I suppose I am in a way," he said. "I am not attached to the regular force. My name is Socrates Smith. You may have heard of me."

To his surprise Jetheroe nodded.

"Yes; I have read your book on blood-tests," he said. "Now, Mr Smith, can I be of any assistance to you? I may tell you that I have never met Mr Mandle, although I know his stepdaughter very well. Very well indeed," he said emphatically.

"Did Miss Templeton come here last night?"

This time the man was obviously master of himself.

"I have not seen Miss Templeton," he said, "for two or three days."

"She didn't come here last night?"

Jetheroe shook his head.

"Why should you imagine she did? I presume she is at Mr Mandle's house. Does she know of this?" he asked.

There was no especial reason why Socrates Smith should think that this man was attempting to deceive him. His voice and his attitude were natural and he answered without hesitation, and yet Soc knew in his bones that this white-haired man was playing with him.

"If you don't mind my saying as much, Mr Jetheroe, you do not seem to be greatly shocked by the death of John Mandle."

"I am not easily shocked," said Jetheroe, leaning back in his chair and putting his fingertips together. "I am neither shocked nor surprised to discover that Mandle has been murdered."

"Why aren't you surprised?" asked Socrates sternly, and a faint smile quivered at the corner of the man's thin mouth.

"Mandle was not the most lovable person in the world," he said. "He treated Molly disgracefully, but that is beside the point. He was an ex-officer of police, and must have made many enemies. For he was a hard, unscrupulous man, who, with his friend Stone, would never hesitate to stretch the limit of fairness in order to secure a conviction against some unfortunate devil who fell into their clutches."

"You seem to know a great deal about him, Mr Jetheroe?"

Jetheroe shrugged his shoulders.

"One learns these things. After all, he was something of a public character in his day, Mr Smith, just as you were."

"Did he ever do you an injury?" asked Soc bluntly, and again that faint smile.

"How could he do me an injury?" replied Jetheroe. "He has only recently swum into my ken. I have been abroad a great deal."

In spite of his imperturbable face and apparent preoccupation, the mind of Socrates Smith was working at whirlwind speed. He put his hand in his pocket aimlessly and took out a little pocketbook.

"I suppose I'd better make a few notes," he said. "Although I am not officially associated with Scotland Yard my presence on the spot is certain to result in my having some official standing in the case."

"Where was he shot?" asked Jetheroe.

"How did you know he was shot?" demanded Soc Smith quickly, and only for a second was the man nonplussed.

"It sounded as though I had some guilty knowledge of the crime," he said with his quick smile. "But I will explain just why I think he was shot. At about half past twelve, or it may have been a quarter to one this morning, I was sitting here working, correcting the proofs of an article I had written for the *Scientific Englishman* – there are the proofs," he pointed to a litter of galley-slips. "In the midst of my work I heard a shot. It came from the direction of the valley. We call that little depression about three hundred yards from the house a 'valley,' though it isn't worthy of the name. I suppose it is called valley because there is a spring, and in the wet season, a little river there."

"Was it one shot you heard?"

"Only one," replied Jetheroe. "I dismissed the matter from my mind, thinking that possibly there were poachers about. When you told me that John Mandle was murdered my mind immediately went back to that shot."

"H'm," said Soc, and opened his notebook.

Standing on a small table at Jetheroe's elbow, he had noticed the remains of a cup of tea and what had evidently been a plate of buttered toast, for one "finger" of toast still remained.

Laying his notebook on his knee Soc wrote three words and Jetheroe watched him keenly.

"Do you know this person?" asked Socrates handing the book to the man.

Jetheroe frowned at the name and shook his head, handing the book back.

"No, I don't know her," he said. "Why?"

"I wondered," replied Socrates and rose, slipping the book into his pocket.

"You are sure you did not see Miss Templeton last night?" he asked softly.

"Absolutely sure," replied the other in an emphatic tone. "I have not seen Miss Templeton for – "

Socrates Smith stooped and drew from under Jetheroe's table a large wastepaper basket, which was half filled with scraps of paper.

He put his hand in and drew something forth. "Will you explain how this came here?" he said, and Lexington gasped, for it was a girl's shoe, and he knew at once that it was the fellow of the one he had discovered in the valley.

THE VANISHING
OF MOLLY TEMPLETON

Only for a second did Jetheroe's mask-like face twitch.

"That is certainly Miss Templeton's shoe," he said, "and its presence here is easily explained. She came over one rainy day and arrived minus a shoe. She said she had lost one in the mud somewhere. It was towards evening and rather dark. I borrowed a pair of old shoes from my housekeeper to send her back in and I made a search for the other. I kept this shoe in my study for some days, and only last night I threw it into the basket, thinking it was very unlikely that the other would be found."

Socrates Smith was silent. As for Lexington, he drew a sigh of relief because the story sounded plausible. But Jetheroe made the mistake of attempting to elaborate the story and offer further explanation.

"Miss Templeton returned the borrowed shoes the next day," he said, "and I hadn't to explain to my housekeeper why I took her property without her knowledge."

"I see," said Socrates. "So that if I questioned your housekeeper on this incident she would know nothing at all about it. Very ingenious. Good morning, Mr Jetheroe."

Jetheroe did not reply. He stood, a silent, watchful figure by the table and made no attempt to escort them to the door.

"Well, what do you think, Soc?" said Lexington as they trudged back to meet the inspector.

"I think Jetheroe is a cold-blooded liar," said Soc cheerfully.

"What was the name you wrote in your book?" Soc chuckled.

"I'll bet you tuppence you'll never guess," he said.

He stopped and opened the book, and reading the name, Lexington's eyebrows went up.

"Why, that is the name of an American film star," he said. "What has she got to do with it?"

"Nothing at all," replied the cheery Soc, his eyes twinkling. "Only did you notice he was eating buttered toast?"

"What the dickens is the connection between buttered toast and Mary Miles Minter?" asked the astonished Lexington.

"However cleanly a man may be, and however carefully he may wipe his fingers, after eating buttered toast," replied Socrates, "he generally leaves a film of grease upon his fingers, and if you look very carefully you will see a thumbprint on the corner. Just turn the book that way so that the sun strikes it at the right angle."

"Do you want his thumbprint?" asked Lexington in astonishment.

"That is exactly what I wanted and that is exactly what I got," said Soc, closing the book carefully and slipping an elastic band about it. "I tell you I am mighty suspicious of gentlemen who go away from this country and remain away for many years. Particularly when nobody seems to know what country they've been living in. Haven't you noticed about genuine travellers and sojourners in distant lands, that the first thing they talk about is the country of their residence, its attractions, its beauties, its hardships or whatever are its characteristics? Take the returned Anglo-Chilian, or the man who has spent years in the Argentine, or Australia, or South Africa. Almost the first information he gives to his new acquaintances is that he knows these countries. When a man comes back after a long absence and is silent or vague about the land in which he has lived, he has either come out of prison or a lunatic asylum, or he is a fugitive from justice from the country of his adoption."

"You're a suspicious old devil," said the admiring Lex. "Do you think Jetheroe knows anything about this murder?"

"Let us ask the inspector what he has discovered," replied Soc.

The inspector had discovered nothing. With the aid of two labourers, who had been commandeered for the purpose, the body of

John Mandle had been lowered to the ground. As Socrates had discovered, it had not been bound and the rope about the body had only the appearance of being fastly tied.

"Now," said Socrates, "we've got the unpleasant job of breaking the news to this poor girl. If you don't mind, inspector, I will go up first."

Inspector Mallett nodded.

"I think it would be wise, sir, and somebody ought to go over to Mr Stone and tell him."

"I'd forgotten Stone," said Soc thoughtfully.

"It will be a great shock to him," the inspector went on. "They were great friends and were together in the police. I suppose you know that."

"Yes," nodded Soc.

He was very silent on the way to the house, and the questions which Lexington put were answered in monosyllables.

The servants were up and about when they returned, and the absence of John Mandle had not been noticed. Timms, his valet, was brushing his clothes when Soc gave him the news. The man went pale and almost collapsed.

"Dead!" he said in a terrified whisper. "Murdered? How? In his room, sir?"

"No, he was murdered at Three Oaks," said Socrates quietly.

"But how could he get there, sir? The poor gentleman couldn't walk."

"You haven't been into his room, of course."

"No, sir. I never go into his room until he rings. He doesn't like being wakened."

"Is Miss Templeton down yet?" asked Socrates.

"I'll ask the maid," said the valet, and disappeared into the servants' quarters. He returned shaking his head.

"No, sir. Miss Templeton doesn't usually get down until about half past nine."

"Let us see Mandle's room first. Ask the maid to wake Miss Templeton and tell her that I have something very important to say to her."

John Mandle's room was a large, airy apartment, the most spacious in the house. It was well but not elaborately furnished. A single bed stood in one corner and it was, of course, empty. More than that, it had not been slept in, as he saw with a glance. He turned to the valet, Timms, who had accompanied the men.

"Didn't you put your master to bed last night?" he asked.

"No, sir," the man shook his head. "Mr Mandle was very particular about that. He always managed to undress himself, though he wanted a little help in dressing."

"Where did you leave him last night?"

"I left him sitting on the edge of the bed just there."

He pointed to a depression where somebody had sat heavily on the edge, near the foot of the bed. The sheets were turned back, the pyjamas, neatly folded, lay on the pillow, but no head had touched the pillow.

"Where does this door lead to?" asked Soc pointing.

"That's a private staircase Mr Mandle had made. It leads down to his study on the ground floor; but he seldom uses it."

Soc tried the door. It was unlocked. The stairway was narrow and dark, and looking round for some means of illumination, he saw a large portable electric lamp standing on a chest of drawers. He took it up and switching on the light made his investigation. The light was particularly brilliant for a battery lamp, but it revealed no clue that made the mystery of John Mandle's extraordinary disappearance any clearer. At the foot of the stairs was another door that was unlocked, and they came into the study which Mandle had built and in which he spent so many hours. His wheelchair stood by the side of his writing table. Soc tried the door leading into the garden. This also was unlocked.

"Curious," he mused. "Very curious. The door has an electric control. I saw the switch by the side of his desk. He would hardly go to bed without having fastened the door in some way or other."

He made a further discovery. Not only was the switch turned to "open," but the second control, which he found by John Mandle's bed in the room above, was also turned to "open."

"Very extraordinary," he said. "What do you want?" – this to an agitated servant.

"I can't get any answer from Miss Templeton's room," she said. "I knocked and knocked. The door is locked."

Socrates Smith went swiftly up the stairs.

"This is the room, sir," said the maid. He tried the door, then, stooping, looked through the keyhole.

"The key is taken out," he said, and knocked again.

"Miss Templeton!" he called loudly.

There was no answer. He put his shoulder against the door and pressed. With a crack the lock broke, and Lexington, who had never before witnessed an exhibition of his brother's remarkable strength, opened his eyes in amazement.

Soc walked swiftly into the room. It was empty!

Here, too, the bed had not been slept in. He came out into the passage and found the valet.

"Timms," he said, "where does Mr Mandle keep his valuables?"

"In his safe, sir," said the man.

"Where is his safe?"

Timms explained that the safe was in what he called the "library," a small apartment at the back of the house to which John Mandle would retire for days when the mood was on him.

The receptacle stood in the corner of the room, a small fireproof safe, and there was no need to ask what had happened; for the door was wide open, and the safe was empty of anything in the shape of valuables.

AT PRINCE'S PLACE

"Had anybody the keys to this safe besides Mr Mandle?" he asked Timms, when he had recovered from the mild shock of the discovery.

"Yes, sir, Miss Molly had keys," said the valet. "I don't think there was anything in the safe of value. Miss Molly used it to keep her account books and her cash for household expenses."

"Nothing else?"

Timms hesitated.

"I believe there was some jewellery there, sir. One of the maids told me once she had seen Miss Molly looking at it, and that Mr Mandle had been very angry with her. Mr Mandle never kept any very large sums of money in the house. When he wanted money I used to go into Godalming to the bank, generally on a Friday."

For ten minutes Socrates paced the lawn, his hands behind him, his chin on his breast; and Lexington, stunned and bewildered by this new turn of events, sat watching him, his unlit pipe in his hand.

"What are we going to do now, Soc?" he asked at last when Soc brought his restless pacings to a halt.

"We're going to have breakfast now," said Socrates Smith brightly. "I've had just as much mystery for the morning as my system will stand."

His breakfast was a hearty one. Lexington scarcely ate a morsel.

"It's the girl that's worrying you," said Socrates, sipping his coffee and looking across the rim at his brother. "You're a darned old sentimentalist, Lex."

"She can't be mixed up in this affair, she can't," protested Lexington. "Do you imagine that a girl like that, with a face – "

"I've known some wonderfully beautiful criminals in my time, Lex," said Soc thoughtfully.

Lex glared at his brother.

"She's no criminal!"

"I'm not saying she is, so you can take that murderous look off your face and remember that violence of any kind is repugnant to me. You look as if, with the slightest encouragement, you'd hit me."

"But, Soc, old boy, it's impossible! Absolutely impossible!" said the other vigorously. "How could she carry a man? – why it's ridiculous."

"How could anybody carry him, for the matter of that, supposing that he didn't want to go?" said Socrates. "At any rate, the mystery of the signal is cleared up."

"Cleared up?"

"Of course; it was Jetheroe signalling to Miss Molly."

"Then you don't believe – ?"

"I certainly don't believe that he hadn't seen her for days. I am equally certain that he saw her yesterday, because those shoes she was wearing were the shoes she wore when we arrived."

Lexington gasped.

"Are you sure?" he said incredulously.

"Absolutely," nodded Soc. "I particularly remember the queer yellow buckles."

Lexington was silent, and the other went on: "Yes, she was at Jetheroe's house last night; for what reason I cannot pretend to explain. She went in response to his signal."

Suddenly a smile dawned in his brother's eyes.

"You're an owl, Soc," he said. "How could he signal her when her room is on the other side of the house?"

This was a blow to Soc's theory.

"That's true," he said thoughtfully. "But why should she have been in her room? She may have been in the garden waiting for that signal."

"She wouldn't have seen it," said Lexington. "You can't see the White House except from the far end of the lawn or from one of these upper windows."

"That upsets one of my hypotheses," admitted the older man. "You're quite right, Lexington, there's the making of a detective in you, though it is a most obvious fact that you discovered. She certainly could not have seen that signal. Now who the devil was Jetheroe dot-dashing to?"

"To Mandle?" suggested Lex, but his brother shook his head.

"I hardly think so. No, that doesn't somehow fit in with my theories. Here comes our inspector, and we have got to explain Miss Molly Templeton's absence."

Lexington frowned.

"Couldn't we say she left for London last night?"

Soc shook his head.

"Does it occur to you," he said quietly, "that Miss Templeton may also be a victim?"

"Good God!" Lexington jumped to his feet, his face white. "You don't seriously suggest that, Soc, do you?"

"It is a possibility which we cannot afford to dismiss. We shall have to tell the inspector all we know."

Twenty-seven years of police service had made Inspector Mallett proof against surprise. He listened to the story of Molly's disappearance without comment until Socrates had finished.

"It's extraordinary," he said. "I've already sent a message into Hindhead and Haslemere, and we will have all the men we can spare to search the country. Then that shoe you found – "

"Was Miss Templeton's. Miss Templeton is Mandle's stepdaughter."

Apparently the inspector did not resent Soc's mild deception, and went off to question Mr Jetheroe.

"Now for the fingerprint," said Socrates, and wrote a hurried letter to Scotland Yard enclosing a leaf torn from his book. "Timms can take this up to London," he said. "Of course, it may be a wholly fruitless enquiry, but one cannot afford to take risks."

"Do you think that Jetheroe is known to the police?" asked Lexington.

"He may be," replied his brother.

He looked at his watch and, to his surprise, it was only a little before nine. What a lot had been crowded into the space of two and a half hours!

"There's nothing to do but wait till the inspector comes back," he told Lexington, and here they had not long to wait.

Inspector Mallett's little car came puffing and blowing up the drive and the inspector jumped out.

"Jetheroe knows nothing," he said, "although his evidence will be important as fixing the hour at which the crime occurred."

"You mean the shot he heard?" asked Soc, and the inspector nodded.

"Has anybody been over to Stone, inspector?"

"No, I haven't had a man to spare yet. I think it wouldn't be a bad idea to go over straight away and tell him myself. Will you come?"

"Can you find room for us all in that car?" asked the sceptical Soc, and the inspector, who was not a little proud of his tiny machine, snorted scornfully, and told a fairy story of having accommodated some seven policemen on the occasion of a burglary which had been committed in the neighbourhood some months before.

"Bob will be terribly upset," said Socrates. "These fellows were life friends, and he won't be a bad bloodhound to put on the trail, for old Bob is the cleverest sleuth I know."

"It is curious Mr Stone getting religious," said Mallett with a grin.

"Has he got it bad?" asked Lex dryly.

"Well, you never know with Mr Stone," said Mallett, skilfully negotiating a big stone that was in the road. "He takes things up and drops them. He hasn't much interest in life, you know: he's a bachelor."

Socrates remembered the sneer of John Mandle about Bob's desire for publicity, but said nothing.

"He's going to address a revival meeting," said the inspector. "His name is printed on bills which are posted all over Godalming. A very jolly gentleman to get religion, isn't he?"

"You can be jolly and pious," said Socrates sententiously.

They swept up a long avenue of pines and came in view of Prince's Place, a much more pretentious building than the modest house which John Mandle had occupied.

"He is a bachelor," said the inspector again, and that was apparently the formula by which he explained not only the eccentricities of his acquaintances but also their opulence.

"I wonder if he is an early riser," said Socrates as he pressed the bell.

Apparently Mr Bob Stone was as dilatory in his rising as his friends. A staid footman said that Mr Stone had not yet rung for his shaving water.

"I must see him at once," said Socrates. "Show me the way to his room."

The man hesitated a moment.

"You are a great friend of Mr Stone's, are you, sir? because he doesn't like being disturbed," and then his eyes fell upon the inspector.

"Good morning, Mr Mallett. I suppose it's all right this gentleman going up? You know Mr Stone is very particular; he doesn't like strangers to come into the house even."

So he was afraid, too, thought Socrates.

"It's all right, Jackson," said Mallett. "These gentlemen are friends of Mr Stone."

The man led the way up the broad flight of stairs and along a wide corridor. At the end was a door.

"This is Mr Stone's room," said the man, and knocked.

There was no reply, and he turned the handle. The door was locked. He knocked again and looked round anxiously at Socrates.

"Is there any other way into the room?" asked Socrates quickly.

"There's a way in through the bathroom here, sir" – he pointed to a smaller door on the right.

This was unlocked and so was the door giving into Bob Stone's bedroom, and Socrates, with a sense of apprehension, turned the handle and walked into the apartment. Then he stopped and stared, for Bob Stone, dressed only in his pyjamas, lay on the bed, a handkerchief tied tightly about his mouth, his hands and his feet knotted firmly together, helpless and glaring!

A BIT OF FLUFF

Socrates tore the bandage from the man's mouth, and with quick fingers tugged at the knots which secured him. In a minute they had lifted him to a sitting position, but he seemed incapable of speech. His face was purple, his wrists were red and swollen, and he sat apparently dazed, rubbing his cramped arms, whilst the four men watched him in silence.

"Well, Bob, what happened?" asked Socrates.

Bob Stone blinked at him.

"What happened?" he said dully. "I don't know what happened. Some men got in here last night and tied me up. I fought like the devil but they were too many for me."

"How many do you think?" asked Soc.

"Three or four. I'm not certain. It was dark. Then they bound me and that's about all I know. I think they had some sort of discussion as to what they were going to do, but something must have disturbed them, for they suddenly disappeared."

"Did you know them?"

Bob shook his head.

"I didn't see them, I tell you."

"What time was this?"

Bob was rubbing his elbow and groaning.

"Curse them," he said. "If I could have only got at my gun – what time, Soc? why, I think it must have been about midnight, or perhaps a little later. I'd been asleep."

It took him some time to recover, and not until he had put on some clothes and had come down to his own comfortable dining-room, did Socrates tell him of Mandle. He was silent during the recital and then dropped his head on his hands and did not speak for a long time.

"It is terrible!" he said. "Terrible!"

"Have you any idea if John had enemies?" asked Socrates.

"We've both had enemies, we've both been threatened."

"By letter?"

Bob Stone nodded.

"But that's a usual experience, as you know, Socrates. You've had the same. About a week ago," he went on, "I had a postcard which unfortunately I have destroyed, telling me to look out for trouble. I took so little notice of it that I chucked the thing into the fire. I have an idea that John was warned at the same time, but he was such a secretive fellow that he would say nothing. I only gathered that he had received such a card by his manner."

When the inspector had gone and they were alone, Soc spoke his mind freely.

"Now see here, Bob, there's nothing to be gained by making a mystery of this business. Both you and John were mortally scared about something."

"How do you know?" asked Bob quickly.

"By the precautions you took. John Mandle had his lawn covered with traps and alarms. You have special burglar alarms on your window which would wake you ordinarily."

Bob Stone's face broadened in a guilty smile. "You're the same old Socrates," he said admiringly. "So you noticed them, did you? Yes, I took reasonable precautions."

"Against whom?"

"Against the Great Unknown." Stone's voice was flippant, and it told the other in so many words that he was not disposed to discuss the matter.

"Do you realize that your Great Unknown was the murderer of John Mandle?" asked Socrates bluntly. Stone was silent for a while.

When he spoke it was in a low tone.

"I will find him in my own way," he said.

Socrates nodded.

"That means that you don't want my assistance."

The man shook his head.

"I won't go so far as saying that," he said, "but I'll find him in my own way."

"Do you know Jetheroe?"

"Jetheroe!" Bob Stone looked up quickly. "The man who lives in the White House? No, I don't know very much about him except that he and Molly are quite good friends. He's a bit of a botanist and Molly is inclined that way too. They met, I think, while she was out on one of her rambles. John never quite approved of the friendship, but I think the girl got more sympathy and kindness from Jetheroe than she ever got from John, who was rather a brute where Molly was concerned."

"You're fond of Molly, aren't you?" The face of Bob Stone twitched.

"Yes, I am," he said quietly. "I suppose it's ridiculous for a man of fifty-four to be in love with a girl of twenty-two or whatever her age is, but I'm very fond of Molly. She is a real nice girl."

"Do you approve of her friendship with Jetheroe?"

"Why not?" asked Bob Stone carelessly. "Have you got anything on Jetheroe?"

"Nothing, except that Molly was at his house last night and has disappeared."

"Disappeared!" Bob Stone jumped up, his face white. "You don't mean that!" he said quickly.

Socrates told him of his search for the girl, of the open safe, the discovery of her shoes. He told him too of the apparition they had seen stealing across the lawn. Bob Stone stared at him.

"The safe is nothing, of course. You don't suppose she'd rob Mandle, do you?" he asked roughly. "She kept some trinkets there of her mother's: probably she took them when she ran away from home. She was always threatening to do it, and it's only natural that she should have gone to Jetheroe, who has been a friend of hers. I wish to heaven – " He stopped.

"That she had come to you?" asked Socrates curiously.

"I was going to say that," replied Bob shortly.

"And now I think I'll have another look at your bedroom," said Socrates. "I can't understand why, having decided to murder John Mandle, they should have been content with just tying you up."

Stone shook his head.

"They probably had the same fate in store for me, but they were disturbed," he said. "It was a perfectly rotten experience, I can tell you, Soc; but go ahead and see what you can find."

The search Socrates made of the bedroom was a very thorough one, and for the greater part of the time he conducted his investigations alone.

"Well," said Stone joining him, "have you found anything?"

"No," replied the other, shaking his head.

"You're a mysterious devil, and if you had you wouldn't say," smiled Bob, who had now recovered from his unpleasant experience, and in this analysis of Socrates Smith's character he was not far out, for Socrates had not told him of the little bit of wet tow, a microscopic strand or two that he had discovered on Bob's pillow, and which was now wrapped carefully in paper in his pocket.

An hour later Socrates Smith sat in Mandle's study, with a small powerful microscope, carefully examining a slide which he had hastily prepared.

"What are you looking at?" asked Lexington, coming into the room.

Soc slipped out the slide, which had been roughly made, and consisted of two slips of glass between which showed a hair-like substance.

"What's this, a little bit of fluff?" asked Lexington.

"A little bit of fluff," said Socrates.

"But what is it?" insisted the other.

"A little bit of fluff," said Socrates again. "I found it on Bob's pillow."

"Left there by the marauder?"

"Left there by the man who trussed Bob so neatly," said Socrates. "Do you know, Lex, this is one of the most fascinating cases I have ever been associated with. I have wired to the Chief Commissioner to ask him if I can take control, but I suppose we shall have one of the young lads of the new school flying down in the course of the day."

This prediction, however, was not to be fulfilled. To his surprise he received authority to go ahead in his investigations.

"By the way," said Socrates — they were lunching at an inn at Hindhead when the telegram had been brought to him — "Bob Stone knows nothing of that little bit of fluff that excited your curiosity, and I don't want him to know, because he would attach the same significance to my discovery as I do, and I don't want to make Bob nervous."

"Is he the kind of man who would get nervous at the threat of danger?"

"You never know," was the cryptic reply.

The police had taken Mandle's body to the mortuary at Haslemere, and the countryside was alive with curious people who were busily destroying whatever tracks the murderers had left. A small battalion of reporters had also arrived, and it was to avoid them that Socrates had taken his lunch away from the house.

Lexington sat through the meal moody and abstracted, and his brother watched him with inward amusement.

"Lex," he said, "you have never had, and it's likely never will have again, so interesting a case under your nose, and you're not a bit excited."

"I'm thinking of something else."

"I know you're thinking of something else," said Socrates dryly, "but she's probably safe in London."

Lexington Smith flushed.

"I can promise you something," drawled Socrates. "Something that will bring the light to your eye and the flutter of hope to your heart."

"Don't rag me, Soc," said the other. "I really am upset about this business. What is it you're going to promise?"

"I promise you that you shall see Molly Templeton tonight," was the unexpected reply.

"Tonight!" gasped Lexington. "Do you know where she is? – are you going to arrest her? – "

"It is not an offence to run away from your stepfather," replied Socrates. "Nor is it a felony to lose your shoe in the mud. No, I don't think anybody has suggested that Miss Templeton has murdered her stepfather, and if they had I should have – "

"I should have broken his infernal neck," said Lexington savagely.

"Well, I wouldn't go as far as that." Socrates was chuckling inwardly. "No, I don't think I should have assaulted him, but I should have been very much amused."

"You're a queer devil, as I've said before," said Lexington, looking at his elder brother in wonder. "Do you know, Soc, I've never seen you on a case like this before. It seems to afford you endless amusement."

"That is because I've a bright young heart," said Soc. "In fact, I'm ever so much younger than you, and if I were a marrying man – " he shook his head. "A girl of character," he said, "and very, very pretty. In fact, I haven't seen a prettier for years."

Lexington's face was painfully red.

"Don't be ridiculous," he said a little stiffly. "I've only known Miss Templeton a few hours. She is a very charming girl and – "

"I know, I know," said his brother quietly, "but if a girl's beauty and charm can make such an impression upon such an old gentleman like myself, what effect must it have upon callow twenty-five?"

He dropped his hand affectionately upon his brother's shoulder.

"You have my blessing," he said solemnly, and Bob Stone, who was standing in the roadway outside the Chequers, heard his laughter, and wondered what there was in that cheerless day which could make any man merry.

They found him waiting for them when they came out of the inn, and the first inquiry was about the girl. He was obviously perturbed and distressed by her disappearance.

"Oh, yes," he said indifferently. "I've been to the Three Oaks and I'm certain it must have been the same gang that attacked me. In the first place, John couldn't walk and would have to be carried."

"What is your theory?" asked Socrates quietly.

"I think that he was attacked in exactly the same manner as I was," said Bob Stone. "They gagged and bound him, got him out of the house and took him down to the place where he was found."

"But why in the tree? Why did they put him in the tree?"

Stone shook his head.

"I've been trying to think of all the criminals I know who have a taste for the bizarre in crime," he said, "and I can't place the man."

"Do you think he was shot before he was put on to the tree?"

"Undoubtedly," said Stone without hesitation.

"Then I don't agree with you."

Stone stared at him.

"You don't agree with me," he said slowly.

"No, I certainly do not," replied Socrates. "The bullet that killed Mandle was fired from the ground upward. If you climbed the tree you would see where the bullet has snapped off several small branches, and if you took the trouble to climb still farther you'd probably be able to trace its course upwards."

Lexington was as surprised as Stone.

"Why should they put him in the tree before they shot him?" he asked, but Socrates shook his head.

"By the way, Bob," he said as they walked down the ride, "the chief has given me a sort of overseeing commission in this business."

"You have charge of the case?" said Stone in surprise. "They don't usually take an outsider."

"Well, I'm hardly an outsider," said Socrates resentfully.

He was sensitive on this point, but apparently Bob Stone did not notice his *faux pas*. He went back from the murder inevitably to the girl.

"I wish to heaven she hadn't gone away at this moment," he said fretfully. "Some sort of suspicion is bound to attach to her, Soc. These fool newspaper reporters will get hold of the story, and we shall have startling headlines – 'Disappearance of the murdered man's daughter' – in tomorrow morning's papers. I've seen Jetheroe," he said suddenly and smiled faintly.

"From your amusement I gather that Mr Jetheroe was rather annoyed by your inquiries?"

Bob nodded.

"Mallett has seen him, and that sort of put his back up."

"Did you get any information from him?"

"None whatever. Of course, she was there last night, but he wouldn't admit it. That fellow is a pretty queer fish. I wish I'd known him before."

They walked on for some time in silence and came to a fork in the road, one branch of which led to the woodlands and the other to the valley. It was the valley road on which Mr Jetheroe's house was sited.

"I wish I'd known him before," said Bob Stone again.

"You've never seen him then?"

Bob Stone shook his head.

"No, he's a stranger to me, and yet there is something curiously familiar about his eyes. I never forget a man's eyes, but I can't place him for the life of me."

He took farewell of them there, and they continued on their way to the house to meet the patient reporters.

"He seems more concerned about Molly than he does about poor John," said Socrates, and looking round at his brother he saw that the boy's face was set and his brows were meeting in an angry frown.

"It's ridiculous!" Lex burst forth. "The idea of a man like that wanting to marry a girl like Miss Templeton – "

"You can call her Molly to me," said Socrates. "I give you my permission."

"But don't you think it's absurd, Soc? Why, he's an old man."

"Nobody is old in this world unless he is dithering," replied Socrates quietly, "and I would only remind you of this unhappy fact, that I am Bob Stone's senior by two years."

"Of course you're not old." The younger man hastened to repair his blunder. "But that fellow! Don't you agree with me that it is monstrous for him even to want to marry her?"

Socrates laughed softly.

"I'm not as shocked as I might be," he said, "and, anyway, she is not very keen on such a marriage, is she?"

"How should I know?" replied Lexington, changing colour, but Socrates did not answer.

"We did, as a matter of fact, have a little talk about things," Lexington went on with an assumption of indifference. "And she told me – well, she hinted that Stone wanted to marry her and that she did not favour the idea."

"Slip it out of your head, Lex," said Socrates seriously as they were turning into the house, "that Stone's desire to marry Molly is a criminal offence. If you ever have serious ambitions to follow my profession, you have to get into the habit of ridding your mind of prejudices. I have no particular desire to serve Stone at this moment. I am merely trying to put you right."

They found half a dozen reporters, all anxious for news, and to these Soc sketched the outline of the story. It is true that he omitted certain important and vital details, but that is a habit into which every police-minded man is liable to get.

He sent the journalists on their way, if not rejoicing, at least contented.

"You did not tell them anything about Jetheroe," said Lex, and Socrates shook his head.

"No, I don't think it would have been wise," he said. "Not only because Jetheroe is material on which I wish to work privately, but also because any investigation in the direction of Jetheroe must switch the enquiry on to Molly Templeton, and that is just what I am anxious to avoid. One fact I discovered from them," he chuckled. "There is a fairly good story of the crime in the early editions of the evening newspapers in London. That is excellent."

"Why?" asked Lexington in surprise.

"Remember to ask me that question tonight," replied Soc.

He spent the afternoon going carefully through all Mandle's documents – all that he could discover. At four o'clock Lexington brought him a telegram.

"The boy has just gone. Is there an answer?" Soc opened the wire, and his brother saw at a glance that it was a long one, for it covered two pages. Socrates read the message slowly and at the end he nodded.

"I thought so."

"What is it?" asked Lexington.

"I will read it," said Socrates. "It is from the Record Department of Scotland Yard. 'Re your message. Thumbprint enclosed is that of Theodore Kenneth Ward. Convicted at the Old Bailey in 1903 for forgery and fraudulent conversion. Sentenced to ten years' penal servitude. He was arrested by Sup-inspector Mandle and Sergeant Stone. On his release from prison in 1910, portion of sentence having been remitted, he was rearrested by Mandle on a further charge of fraud, and was sentenced to three years' penal servitude.' "

The two men looked at one another.

"Well, that's Jetheroe," said Socrates grimly.

WHO WAS JETHEROE?

The blue dusk lay in the valley, and the sun had gone to rest behind the Devil's Punch Bowl when Stone made his reappearance. He looked haggard and tired, and fell heavily into the chair which Lexington pushed forward.

"There is no trace of her anywhere," he said. "Neither at Haslemere nor at Godalming has she been seen, and none of the railway officials remember her leaving. She is known at both places, so the stationmasters tell me."

Socrates nodded.

"I didn't imagine she'd leave by train," he said. "She went by bicycle at about five o'clock this morning."

Stone stared at him.

"How do you know?" he asked.

"I am only guessing at the time, but I should think about an hour after sunrise saw her on her way."

"But she hadn't a bicycle! John Mandle would never have given her the money for one."

"Somebody else gave it to her," said Socrates. "At any rate, she could ride a bicycle. I have taken the liberty of going through her bureau this afternoon and I have found amongst other things a broken bicycle pump, nearly new, which she had evidently been repairing in secret. This, and other evidence, proves that she was a cyclist, and the balance of probability is that she kept her machine elsewhere than at the house."

"Where do you suggest?" asked Stone shortly.

51

"At Jetheroe's! He was a friend of hers. He probably supplied the machine. I looked very carefully this morning for tracks on the road, but there were too many in the vicinity of Jetheroe's house for me to be absolutely sure that her machine had passed that way today. Besides," he went on with a smile, "there's no mystery about her cycling. Mallett has seen her on the Haslemere Road, and, apparently, the only people who did not know she was in the habit of taking a spin were you and John Mandle."

Stone was silent. He sat, his head bent and his hands clasped together, studying the pattern of the carpet.

"Jetheroe seems to have been very much in her confidence," he said moodily.

"Do you remember Jetheroe?"

"Do I remember him?" Stone looked up.

"Do you remember a man named Ward, Theodore Kenneth Ward?"

"Good Lord, that's not Jetheroe?" said Stone springing to his feet. "Yes, I remember him very well. Of course, it's Ward! The man whom Mandle hated so much! I've never seen Mandle so relentless as he was in piecing together the case against Ward, especially the second case. Mandle had left the force and actually got the case together at his own expense. When he found Ward only received a sentence of three years, he was the maddest man I've ever known. You must remember the trial!"

Socrates nodded.

"I recall it now," he said.

"So Jetheroe is Ward, eh?" said Stone, and his eyes narrowed. "I wonder why he came to live in this neighbourhood," he said thoughtfully. "Of course, he'd have money planted."

"What is the story of Ward, and why did Mandle hate him?" asked Soc.

"I've never understood," replied the other shaking his head. "I've always thought there was a woman in it, and I think so still. Ward was a man who had been engaged for some years in a series of frauds, and Mandle worked up the case that got him ten years. There is no doubt that the fellow was a brilliant swindler. It is also certain that Ward was not the only name under which he traded. Every effort we made to trace him in his private life failed. I've often wondered," he mused, "whether Mandle, in making his search, came upon Ward's family. There was some talk of his having a very pretty wife who was wholly ignorant of her husband's career of crime." He knit his brow in an effort of memory. "It was Mandle who told me that," he nodded. "Of course, it was Mandle! I wonder!"

Socrates did not interrupt his thoughts, and presently Bob Stone spoke again.

"Three years after Ward went down, Mandle surprised us all by marrying a widow with a child. A beautiful woman was Mrs Mandle. You probably never knew her, did you, Soc?"

Socrates shook his head.

"Suppose – " said Stone softly.

"That Mrs Mandle was Jetheroe's wife?"

Bob Stone nodded.

"It's not a fantastic theory. If she was ignorant of her husband's career, she was also ignorant of his fate. Mandle would stick at nothing to get what he wanted, and it is just as likely as not that he faked some story of this man's death after so long an absence. In fact, that he persuaded Mrs Ward to marry him whilst her husband was still living."

"But how did she get the name Templeton?"

"That may have been one of Ward's aliases," said Bob. "It is an interesting theory."

"And if it is accurate," said Socrates, "it means that Molly Templeton is Ward's daughter."

"Good God! So it does!" gasped Bob Stone. "So it does!"

"Incidentally," said Socrates, "it supplies a very strong and sufficient motive for the murder of John Mandle."

A dead silence followed his words.

"Yes, there's the motive all right," said Stone at last, "a motive, a real motive."

He rose unexpectedly.

"I'm going for a walk to think this out," he said. "You will let me know if you hear anything about Molly?"

Lexington broke his long silence.

"You told me to repeat a question I put to you earlier in the day. Soc," he said, "why were you glad that the news of this murder was in the evening newspapers?"

There was a little commotion in the hall and the maid came in, her face glowing.

"Miss Templeton is back!" she gasped.

"That's the reason," said Socrates, but Lex was out of the room in two strides and was babbling incoherently to the white-faced girl in the hall.

MOLLY TELLS HER STORY

"Is it true, is it true?" she was asking. "Oh, say it isn't true! Is – " she hesitated before the word "father" Socrates noticed. He nodded gravely.

"I'm afraid it's too true, Miss Templeton," he said.

"And that story about – about the tree, is it true?"

He nodded again.

"I can't understand it. It is too terrible!"

She offered her hand to Bob Stone, who came out to them, and Lex observed with jealous interest that the man held her hand and did not let it go.

"I suppose you saw the account in the evening newspapers and that brought you back?" said Socrates.

"I saw it quite by accident," replied the girl. "Of course, it was in all the late papers, but only one paper had the account in the earlier editions, and that was the one I saw."

Socrates took her arm and led her back into the drawing-room.

"I think you can tell us a lot, Miss Templeton," he said, but she shook her head.

"I can't tell you very much."

And then he saw a strange look on her face.

"I wonder?" she said half to herself.

"What do you wonder?"

"I'd better tell you the story from the beginning," she said, and took off her hat.

It was Lexington who took it from her hand and helped her off with her cloak, a defiant Lexington, thought Socrates, secretly amused, though Bob Stone did not seem to realize the challenge which the younger man was throwing out.

"After you went to bed last night, Mr Smith," she said, "father asked me to stay and talk to him. I called him 'father' though I had no feeling for him that a daughter could have or should have. He was very harsh with me. I don't want to speak ill of him now, God knows, but he did not make life particularly pleasant. About two years ago I met a gentleman who lives in this neighbourhood, an elderly man, who was very kind to me. I had practically the run of his house."

"Mr Jetheroe, of course," interrupted Socrates, and she inclined her head.

"He bought me a bicycle — you know that probably." There was the faintest smile in her eyes, a tribute to Socrates and the thoroughness of his investigations. "I had to keep it very quiet from Mr Mandle or there would have been trouble. But as I was saying, Mr Mandle asked me to stay behind after you had gone to bed and gave me a terrible bullying about — about — " her face went scarlet, and Socrates knew that the subject of the acrimonious discussion was the girl's attitude toward Lexington — "well about something that didn't concern him. I told him I would leave the house, and he said I could leave at once. I went up to my room and changed, and then I made my way out of the house across the lawn."

"I saw you," said Socrates.

"You saw me?" she said in surprise. "You were looking out of the window?"

"We were both looking out of the window," smiled Soc. "But I interrupt you."

"The only place I thought of going was across to Mr Jetheroe. He told me that if ever I wanted to run away I was to come straight to him, and he would give me the means of getting a living."

"One moment," interrupted Soc again. "Did you have any system of signals?"

"Signals?" she said puzzled.

56

"Between you and Mr Jetheroe?"

She shook her head.

"I don't know what you mean."

"I mean do you understand the Morse code and the use of the flash lamp?"

"No," she smiled, "I have never studied telegraphy."

"And you have never signalled to him?"

"No," she said in surprise.

"Nor he to you?"

"Not that I'm aware of. If he had it would have meant nothing to me, because I shouldn't have understood it."

"All right; go on," said Socrates. "What happened next?"

"I got to the road and then started down the path which leads into the valley and is the nearest way to Mr Jetheroe's house. I'm not at all nervous for I have made that journey hundreds of times, but last night I had a queer feeling that I was being watched."

"Let me see," said Socrates, "how long was it after you had left your father – Mr Mandle – that you went away from the house?"

"It must have been half an hour," said the girl.

Socrates nodded.

"You thought you were being watched?"

"I am certain I was being watched," she said emphatically. "I could have sworn I saw a man skulking in the bushes and I heard a footstep behind me and started to run. I got off the path near the spring and lost my shoe, but I didn't stop to look for it."

"Mr Jetheroe was not in bed, I presume?"

"No, he was up," said the girl. "In fact, he answered the door himself."

She stopped suddenly.

"I don't know whether I ought to tell you all this? Have you seen Mr Jetheroe?"

Socrates nodded.

"And of course he has done his best to shield you because he did not want us to know where you had gone."

"I spent the night on the sofa in his study," she said, "and he woke me at four o'clock with a cup of tea, and at five o'clock I took my bicycle out of the shed and rode to London. He gave me money to get lodgings and the address of some people he knew in business and who would help me to get work," she smiled. "You don't know how good Mr Jetheroe is. He wanted to give me an allowance so that I didn't work at all, and was terribly upset when I refused. Now I am going upstairs to change. Is – is – " she hesitated, and Socrates knew what she meant.

"No, he has been taken into Haslemere," he said.

"Well, what do you think of it?" asked Stone when she had gone.

"Her story is of course true."

"True?" said Stone indignantly, and here for the first time Lexington found himself in sympathy with the ex–detective. "Of course it's true! You never for one moment thought she would lie, did you?"

"I think anybody can lie," said Socrates coolly. "It is one of the accomplishments which are common to humanity. And she thought that she never saw Mandle alive again after she left him in the drawing-room!" he said musingly.

"Well, neither did she if she says so," said Lexington.

"She saw him again." Socrates looked at him strangely. "She saw him again," he said slowly, "but she did not know it was he. For the man who was skulking in the bushes when she passed was John Mandle!"

Soc's statement struck his hearers dumb.

"You're mad," said Stone at last. "How could it have been Mandle – Mandle who couldn't walk!"

"Nevertheless, it was John Mandle," insisted Socrates.

"Are you suggesting there was a miracle last night?"

"There were two miracles last night," said Socrates lighting a long black and very evil-smelling cigar, "both of which are susceptible to a very simple explanation, but what that explanation is I'm not prepared for the moment to say – because – "

"Well?" they asked in unison.

"Because I don't know," said Socrates with a broad smile. "Stone, you'll stay to dinner?"

He avoided Lex's eyes with their anguished appeal and was oblivious to the unmuttered curses which his brother was pouring on his head.

"Thank you, I will," said Stone. "You'll stay here till this business is through?"

Socrates nodded.

Later, pacing to and fro in solitary meditation, Socrates was joined by his brother.

"What the devil did you ask that fellow to stay for?" grumbled Lexington, and almost for the first time in his life the eyes which Soc turned upon his brother were very cold.

"Do you regard Bob Stone as such an overwhelmingly favoured rival that you dare not compete with him?" he asked sharply. "Does it occur to you, Lex, that I want Bob here for the assistance he may give me, and that the solution of this Three Oaks mystery is a much more important matter to me and to the world in general than that you should lose or gain an opportunity of meeting Molly Templeton?"

Lex hung his head.

"I'm sorry, old man," he said in a low voice, and then the arm of Socrates was round his shoulder.

"Love is an amiable form of lunacy," he said. "Now shut up and leave me alone. I've got seven separate problems which have to be settled in my mind before I go any further."

He was late for dinner, and the girl, who had come to the table with a new piece of information to give him, waited impatiently for his appearance. When he did come he was more serious than Lex had ever seen him, and sat through the first two courses without speaking a word save to answer as shortly as possible any question that came to him.

"Have you found Mr Mandle's diary?" she asked at last, toward the end of the meal.

"I didn't know he kept a diary," said Socrates quickly, and his air of preoccupation fell away like a cloak.

"I only discovered it this afternoon," she said.

"I don't know whether I'm right in describing it as a diary, but Timms, who was admitted to the study, told me that he thought it must be a diary, because Mr Mandle was writing in a book. He said there were two whole books full of closely written matter, and it was all about Mr Mandle's own life, because he had seen the beginning of a page in the wastepaper basket and had remembered the words. There was only one line on the page, and it had apparently been discarded because of a grammatical error. The words were: 'About this time we began to feel that Deveroux – ' "

"Deveroux?" said Soc quickly. "That was the Lyons Bank man that Mandle let slip."

"Say Mandle and I," said Stone laconically; "but it made a deeper impression upon Mandle than upon me. What was he doing, I wonder, writing the story of his life? It would have been an interesting life, anyway." He nodded. "Was there anything more?"

The girl shook her head.

"I've searched the desk very thoroughly," said Socrates. "I wonder if there's a secret drawer; it is an old-fashioned kind of desk that is likely to have – " he stopped suddenly, switching round to the door.

The door was ajar, and soft though the footfall had been he had heard a movement. He rose to his feet, gripped the handle of the door and jerked it open. A man stared in the entrance, a grey-haired man.

"Good evening, Mr Jetheroe," said Socrates politely, "and how did you get in?"

FIRE!

But Jetheroe was neither looking at him nor paying the slightest attention to what he was saying. His eyes were fixed on the girl, and a smile of singular beauty softened and illuminated the rugged face. She came halfway across the room to meet him with outstretched hands.

"So you've got back. I thought you would come," he said. "I have been worried about you today, and I'm afraid I had to tell a lot of fairy stories to these gentlemen."

"I am so glad you came over," she said, looking at him with shining eyes. "I didn't know how to tell you I was back. I couldn't have come across to see you tonight," she said and shuddered.

"So I thought," he said calmly. "I must apologize to you for interrupting this meal; and answering your question, Mr Smith, I came through the front door, which was open."

There was a certain note of challenge in his voice, as though he were demanding from Socrates his authority for questioning his presence. And in truth, whilst Molly was in the house, she was its mistress, and Socrates had no right whatever to ask a guest why or by what means he came. This fact he admitted to himself and as readily admitted to the visitor.

"I've got into the habit of thinking that I own the place," he said good-humouredly, "and I am merely adding to my impertinence by inviting you to sit down. Do you know Mr Stone?"

"We have met before," said Jetheroe, "in London some sixteen or eighteen years ago. Mr Stone, do you remember?"

61

Bob Stone nodded, and Socrates realized that his knowledge of Jetheroe's past had lost half its potency by the tacit confession made in the man's speech.

"I really came over," said Jetheroe, seating himself at the girl's invitation, "to ask you whether you would like to stay with me at my house tonight. I hardly think you'd care to be here."

She hesitated.

"I don't particularly want to stay here tonight," she said, "but I can get a room at the Chequers. I asked about one on my way here, and they are reserving it."

He nodded.

"I think you're wise," said Bob Stone. "You're very wise, in fact."

Jetheroe was looking from one to the other at the table, and again that sweet smile of his lit up his countenance.

"I am afraid I came at an unpropitious moment and interrupted an interesting discussion," he said as he rose. "Good night, Molly."

"Good night, Mr Jetheroe." She held his hand in both of hers.

He did not go alone. Bob Stone went with him, to Lexington's undisguised relief. Before he went he took Socrates aside.

"Soc," he said in a low voice, "I'll come over tomorrow and help search for that diary or life of John's. Maybe it will throw a light upon a good many things which are now a little mysterious. I'd stop tonight and help you, but I think you want the light of day for that business."

"We'll get the desk out into the garden and cut it to pieces – "

"You don't think that it's hidden anywhere else?"

Socrates shook his head.

"I've made a most careful search," he said.

"I am inclined to the theory of the secret drawer. The desk is one of those big cumbersome pieces of furniture which must be simply honeycombed with cavities."

Bob nodded.

"I'll be with you at half past nine. Is that early enough?"

He looked round over his shoulder at the girl.

"I suppose Molly doesn't want to go to the inn yet," he said.

"I'll take her there when she does," said Socrates, hypocritically, for he knew that when the time came, there would be only one escort for Miss Molly Templeton.

He left the young couple alone whilst he continued his examination of the papers which John Mandle had left. They were mostly of an uninteresting character, and he found amongst them no evidence of this life story which Timms had seen him writing. He had a good look at the desk, tested some of the drawers, and looked for the conventional secret cupboards but without success. It would be a long job, he thought, but it might easily yield the most surprising secrets.

He looked at his watch, and was amazed to find it was eleven o'clock.

"I say, you people," he said, going into the drawing-room, "do you know what the time is? Your hotel will be closed."

"I am going to stay here tonight, I have decided," said the girl a little breathlessly. Socrates looked from one to the other in wonder.

It was youth. Youth fundamentally callous and indifferent to all else but the chief process of life. Youth courting in the house of death, an amazing phenomenon brought home to Socrates Smith for the first time in his life. He scratched his head and laughed softly.

"What is amusing you, Soc?"

"Just thoughts," said Socrates. "Now, Miss Templeton, I'm going to be your uncle and send you to bed."

She was a little confused.

"I didn't know it was so late," she said penitently. "Good night, Mr Smith. Good night, Lexington."

" 'Lexington!' " thought Socrates.

It was apparently necessary for Molly Templeton's peace of mind that Lex should accompany her to the foot of the stairs. They must have been talking on matters of such tremendous import that the scene could not be suspended until the last possible moment.

"Well, Lex," said Socrates when his brother had returned. "Have you settled the affairs of the world?"

"Of my world," said Lexington boldly.

Socrates raised his eyebrows.

"Are you starting a world, too?" he asked sardonically. "A world for two, eh? And the rest of humanity are to be picturesque items on the landscape. She's a very nice girl, Lex."

"She's the best girl in the world," said Lex.

"I wouldn't say that," rejoined his brother, "though I daresay she's somebody's nicest girl in the world. Now you can go to bed."

"Have you finished your work?" asked Lexington, glad to jump the subject of Molly Templeton.

"For the night. We are going to get the old desk out tomorrow and turn her inside out. I wonder if Jetheroe heard?"

"When he was outside the door?"

Socrates nodded.

"We were talking about secret drawers and things."

"Do you think he is interested?" asked Lexington.

"I don't know," said Socrates shortly. "Off you go to bed, my son. An early morning for you."

Lexington paused on the stairs and turned round.

"By the way you're clearing your throat and are trying to balance yourself on one foot, I gather that you've already arranged another walking partner for the morning," said Socrates; "and you're welcome, because I've got quite a lot of work to do."

He went into his room, and presently Lexington, who was on the point of getting into bed, heard a tap at his door.

"Come in," he said.

It was Socrates.

"I've an idea. A brainwave, Lex. Put on your dressing-gown and come with me into Mandle's room. You're not scared, are you?"

"Not a bit," said Lexington stoutly, though he had felt a momentary qualm.

The girl's room was at the other end of the passage, so that they had not to pass it. To his surprise, Socrates did not switch on the light when they went into the room, but felt for, and found, the electric lamp with which he had found his way down to the study.

"This is the fellow I want to see."

He pulled a little table to the window, which was open.

Laying the lamp on the table he touched a switch and a bright gleam of light shot out.

"Now go into my room and tell me what you see," said Socrates.

Lexington obeyed. From the window he could see the White House.

"Great heavens!" he said aloud, for the windows of the White House were illuminated with the dull glow which they had seen on the earlier night!

He made his way back to Socrates and told him.

"I thought so," said Soc quietly. "What we thought was a signal from the White House was merely the reflection of this lamp in the big windows."

"Then Mandle was signalling?"

Soc nodded.

"But to whom?"

"I don't know," replied Socrates.

He went back to his own room with a curt goodnight to his brother.

Lexington sat for a long time at his window before he finally fell into bed, to doze and soon to sleep.

And then he began to dream. He dreamt he was in France and that the enemy were making a night attack. He could hear the crash of the machine-gun fire, caught the gleam of bursting shells, and choked in the poisonous fumes that rolled across No-man's-land. Then one of the enemy, a big officer with a face like Jetheroe, grappled with him and he struck out wildly.

"Wake up, wake up," said the officer, shaking him by the shoulder, and he blinked open his streaming eyes.

It was Socrates.

"Wake up, Lexington! The house is on fire!"

"What?"

"The house is on fire," said Socrates quickly. "Get Miss Templeton out of her room. Break in the door if necessary. I am going to see that the servants are aroused."

"Fire?" said Lexington dully.

Then he heard the crackle of wood burning fiercely, saw flames and the rolling yellow smoke. The room was full of it, the passage was thick with it. He groped his way along the corridor and knocked at the girl's door. There was no answer, and without waiting any further he smashed in the panels, turned the key through the hole he had made, and staggered into the room.

She was lying half in and half out of bed, he saw, when he could see anything. And she had a book in her hand – but this he did not see. A fat leather-bound book, the covers fastened together with a lock. The fire was raging in the rooms beneath them, and the room was blisteringly hot. She must have been overcome by the smoke, for she made no sign of life when he lifted her in his arms and carried her back along the passage, now red with the flames that had broken through from beneath.

The door of Mandle's room was burning, and two or three rooms were alight below, but fortunately the stairway had not yet caught. The hall was black with smoke, but the door was wide open.

Socrates, with a little knot of servants, was standing in the doorway peering into the gloom.

"Here you are, thank God!" he said, when Lex appeared with his burden. "Timms, there are some coats hanging in the hall, do you think you can get them?"

"I'll have a try, sir," said Timms, and dashed into the building.

He emerged presently, his two arms full of wraps, and only just in time, for they had not been a few seconds clear of the building before the floors gave way and a volume of flame shot up and cut through the shingled roof as if it were paper.

It was fully five minutes before the girl recovered consciousness and found herself wrapped in an old overcoat of John Mandle's. She looked about her in bewilderment.

"What has happened?" she asked. "Oh, yes, I remember – the fire," she said shakily. "I tried to get out of bed, but I must have fainted."

"You were technically gassed," said Socrates, who by great good luck had retrieved his own overcoat and had found his cigar-case in his pocket. "It's a pretty thorough fire, too," he said, watching the doomed building, now a roaring inferno. "The nearest fire brigade is in Haslemere," he said, "and they'll arrive in time to lay the foundation stone of the new building. Whoof! It's hot here!"

"Where did it break out?" asked the girl, now able to stand with the assistance of Lex's encircling arms.

"I don't know," replied Socrates puffing steadily at his cigar. "Everywhere I should say."

"Do you think it was a fuse – ?" she began.

He shook his head.

"If I hadn't been the biggest fool in the world," he said bitterly, "there would have been no fire."

He did not explain in what manner his folly was responsible. The maligned fire brigade arrived much sooner than they expected, but too late to render any assistance. Fortunately the girl's room at the inn was booked and the village was aroused. They had no difficulty in getting her to safety and finding rooms for themselves.

Socrates Smith did not go to bed. Dressed in a pair of breeches several sizes too large for him and a shooting-coat, the arms of which were at least six inches too short, he spent a busy night telephoning.

When Lex came down the next morning he found his brother, by diligent searching, in the hands of the local barber.

"I've phoned the excellent Septimus to bring some clothes down," he said, "and the fire department are sending their best expert."

"Why?" asked Lex in surprise.

"Because I am a most inquisitive man," said Socrates, "and I want to know just where that fire started! And do you know where it started, Lex?"

Lex shook his head.

"I thought you didn't either," he said.

"It is only a speculation," said Socrates, "but I'm willing to bet you three hats to one that it started on Mandle's desk, the desk with the secret drawers. I am willing to bet also," he went on slowly, "that the expert finds evidence of petrol not only there but in all the downstairs rooms."

67

"Good God!" said Lex shocked, "do you mean it is a case of arson?"

"That's the lady," said Socrates, and when the experts came and they accompanied him in a search through the still smoking ruins they had confirmation of Soc's suspicion.

"The fire started here," said the gentleman from London, pointing to the debris of John Mandle's study. "This was a desk, I presume."

"That was a desk."

The expert stooped and sniffed.

"Petrol was used. It's curious you can't destroy the smell of petrol, and I sniffed it in the other part of the building, too. Was there anything inflammable in the desk?"

"There was," replied Socrates grimly.

He had bought a hatchet in the village, and now he began gently to chop at the charred remnants of the desk. There was no sign of unburnt paper. The fire had been very thorough, though he discovered the secret drawer and presumably the ashes of John Mandle's last manuscript. It was burnt to a cinder, and, moreover, a piece of burning wood had fallen upon the cinders and had reduced them to powder, so that it was impossible to decipher one word after another.

But one discovery he did make. A blow from his hatchet laid bare a receptacle which was only partially burnt and at the bottom lay two keys, a large old-fashioned key and a smaller one.

"Hello, what are these?" asked Socrates.

Attached to the bigger key was a brass label on which was stamped: "Garden Gate."

To the other was a paper label which was half-burnt, the rest so discoloured that it was some time before he could make out the writing. "Pool in – th – "

"Pool in the – what?" he asked.

The expert smiled.

"One doesn't as a rule have a key to a pool," he said pleasantly, and passed on to show other indications that the fire might have been started simultaneously at half-a-dozen points.

"I should think, though, it started here," he said; "every bit of this wood is saturated with petrol, and there is petrol on the floor and petrol on what looks to be a flight of wooden stairs."

Socrates had dropped the keys in his pocket and was now taking no more than an academic interest in what the expert said.

After all, it was only confirmation of his own suspicions, suspicions that amounted to certainties, that he was hearing.

" 'Pool in the' what?" he said as he walked back to the inn with Lexington. "By the way, don't let us talk about these keys even to Miss Templeton."

"Righto," said Lexington, who had other matters to discuss with Molly Templeton of infinitely greater interest to himself and, as he hoped, to her.

WHAT GRITT HEARD

They found Bob Stone had arrived when they got back to the hotel. He was with the girl in the private sitting-room which Socrates had engaged, and his face was troubled.

"It makes me go cold to think about it." More and more he was assuming a proprietorial attitude toward the girl, thought Lexington.

"I wish to heaven you hadn't had this experience, Molly. You told me you were going to the hotel," he said reproachfully.

She laughed.

"It was an extraordinary experience," she said. "Terrible though it was, I am glad I have had it."

"Was anything saved?" asked Bob Stone.

"Nothing," said Socrates shaking his head. "It was a very thorough burn up. The only place left standing is the summer house at the end of the garden."

The girl shook her head sorrowfully.

"Poor Mr Mandle. He loved the summer house. He spent hours there."

"How did it happen?" asked Stone.

"Some petrol caught fire," replied Soc.

"Was it the garage?"

Soc shook his head.

"The garage suffered with the rest of the building, but the fire started in one of the downstairs rooms; to be exact, in the study; to be more exact, on the desk with the secret drawers where John Mandle's life story was hidden."

Bob stared at him.

"Do you mean it was a case of arson?" he said.

"I mean just that," replied Socrates.

"But who – " began Bob.

"Who killed John Mandle?" interrupted Socrates quietly. "A man who would deliberately murder another, would as deliberately destroy evidence which might betray him. Incidentally destroy an eminent worker in the cause of good law who was doing his poor best to unravel Mandle's death."

Bob did not speak till the girl had gone out of the room.

"Are you going to arrest Jetheroe?" he asked quietly.

"Why do you think it is Jetheroe?"

"Because Jetheroe was outside the door when we were discussing this secret drawer and the life of John Mandle," replied Bob Stone. "Because Jetheroe is one of the few men in England who have genuine cause to hate John, and because he lived in such a position that he could, better than any other, destroy the man he hated."

Socrates scratched his chin thoughtfully.

"Did John Mandle ever discuss Jetheroe? Did he know he was living in the neighbourhood?"

"He knew he was there," replied Bob. "But he had no idea who he was any more than I had. He objected to Molly associating with him, but he did not put his foot down as I should have expected. Probably he thought Jetheroe was an older man than he is. He conveys the impression of great age."

"It's a rum business." Socrates shook his head. "No, I'm not applying for a warrant."

Stone was thinking deeply, his eyes fixed on the ground.

"Did you notice last night that Jetheroe was rather insistent upon Molly staying at his house, and was satisfied when he learnt that she was going to the hotel?"

"So were you for the matter of that," smiled Socrates. "What do you suggest?"

"I suggest Jetheroe knew there was going to be a fire at 'The Woodlands' last night," said Bob Stone quietly, "and he was anxious for the girl to be out of the way. Remember, if our theories are correct, Molly is his daughter."

Socrates was silent.

"Has he been up this morning?" he asked.

"No, but he has seen Molly. He met her at the draper's, where she was buying some things."

"Why didn't he come up last night? He must have seen the fire from his house."

Again Socrates smiled.

"All your suspicions are a little wild, Bob," he said. "One might say why didn't you come up, because 'The Woodlands' is visible from your place."

"I did come up," said Bob Stone with a laugh. I arrived just after you'd gone to the hotel. The firemen told me, but I had not the slightest idea that Molly was with you, and I didn't want to disturb you. No, the net seems to be working round Jetheroe, and if I were in your place, Soc, I should pull him in."

Again Socrates scratched his chin, and it was not like him to show any signs of uncertainty.

"The whole thing wants a tremendous lot of thinking over," he said. "Are you going to the inquest tomorrow?"

Bob nodded.

"The funeral is in the afternoon," said Socrates. "Poor old John, what a queer end to a queer career! By the way, you knew him much better than I. Had he any other house in the country?"

Bob shook his head.

"No," he said, "why do you ask?"

"Had he a place in London? Did he go in for real estate?"

"I've never heard about it," said Bob. "He was not a man to talk much about his business, but I think he would have spoken of that. Why?"

"Because," said Socrates, "I should like to know exactly what I am going to do with Molly."

Bob nodded.

"I see your idea. You mean she ought to go away. I think it a good notion. But I'm afraid he hasn't any other property. I am quite willing to turn out of Prince's Place and go to London to live if she would accept that, but she has turned down my suggestion."

"She couldn't very well take it," said Socrates quietly.

"But there is no reason why all of you shouldn't come," said Bob quickly. "She wouldn't mind if you were there, and – and if the visit is prolonged I could get a lady to join the party, too."

Socrates nodded.

"That would make it possible. I will speak to Molly." Then: "Bob, are you very keen on her?"

The question was so unexpected that it left the other speechless.

"What – what do you mean?" he asked.

"Do you want to marry her?" asked Socrates bluntly.

"Yes, I do," this after a momentary pause. "I am very fond of her, Soc."

"And how does she feel about it?"

"She – doesn't like it," replied the other, and abruptly changed the subject.

The girl joined them soon after. Yes, she had seen Mr Jetheroe. He had come down to the draper's, which was also the local employment bureau, to hire another gardener. His own gardener had been dismissed that morning for drunkenness – his fourth offence.

"I know the man," nodded Bob, "a shiftless fellow who used to work for Mandle. Gritt. Isn't that the man?"

"I think that is the name," said the girl. "I didn't take much notice."

"Was Mr Jetheroe very much agitated when he learnt that you had had such a narrow escape?" asked Socrates.

"Why, of course," said the girl in surprise. "He was terribly upset. He thought I was staying at the inn."

"I see," nodded Soc.

He had to drive to Haslemere Station soon after, to meet two detectives who had been sent down from Scotland Yard, and had been placed under his instructions. He came back to the Chequers about five o'clock. A fine rain was falling. The girl was out. She had gone to the White House to take tea with Jetheroe, and to his surprise, Socrates learnt that the faithful Lexington had accompanied her.

He grinned sympathetically, but it was an inside grin because Bob Stone, who gave him the information, was not in the best of humours.

"That brother of yours is a bit of a fly-by-night, isn't he, Soc?" he asked.

"Both by day and by night," said Socrates calmly, "and wherever he flies, he flies straight, Bob."

"I'm not saying anything against him," growled the other, "but I'm a bit tender on the point of Molly."

"Bob, you're a fool to worry about a girl at your time of life. When fifty-five marries twenty-two there's liable to be a whole century between them by the time they're ten years older."

Bob Stone licked his lips.

"I suppose you're right, Soc," he said. He was going to say something else when the waitress came in.

"Would you see Mr Gritt, sir?" she asked, addressing Soc. "He says he's got something important to say."

"Show him in," said Socrates.

"He's not quite himself, you know, sir," she said hesitatingly.

"Do you mean he's rather drunk?" asked Socrates amused. "Nevertheless, show him in."

The man came in, a spare gaunt figure, bent of shoulder, with an unpleasantly shifty look in his eyes.

He stood fingering his cap by the door till Socrates nodded to him to be seated.

"Well, Gritt, what do you want?"

"What's the reward for this murder?" asked Gritt. He had evidently been drinking, and his voice was husky and unsteady.

"There is no reward offered, if you mean for the detection of the murderer," replied Socrates, "but a reward is usually given to any man who lays information which will bring about a conviction."

"All right," said Gritt viciously, "then I'm going to get the reward, for I know who did it."

"You know who did it?" Bob Stone leant across the table and asked the question eagerly.

"Yes, I do," replied the man truculently. "Who said I don't?"

"Who was it?" asked Socrates.

"My old governor. Mr Jetheroe – and I can prove it," said Gritt.

If he expected to produce a sensation he was not disappointed. Bob sat back in his chair with a little gasp. Socrates' eyes seemed to grow visibly brighter.

"Oh yes," he said softly, "and you can prove this."

"Of course I can!" said Gritt. "I know what happened, anyway, and I know what he said! It was after the young lady came. I was cleaning the boots in the little tool-shed – "

"Rather late for boots," interrupted Socrates.

"Well, I ought to have done them before," confessed the man, "but I was up at the Red Lion having a drink with some friends of mine – "

"I understand," said Soc; "well, tell me what happened. This was the night before last you're speaking about?"

The man nodded.

"Yes, sir, it was the night before last. I was just carrying the boots up to the house when I saw the young lady come in. She was sort of limping, I don't know why."

Evidently he had not heard of the missing shoe, and neither Socrates nor Bob enlightened him on the subject.

"She went in, and was there about ten minutes when the governor came out. I was on my way back to the tool-shed with the boots, because the cook had locked the kitchen door and I couldn't get in, and the way I was walking brought me quite close to the front door – in fact he passed me so near that I could have put out my hand and touched him on the shoulder. I didn't though," he added humorously, and laughed at his joke.

"Well?" said Socrates.

"Well, I went back to the tool-house. I had a bottle of beer in there, and I sat down and had a drink thinking over things, and presently I thought I'd better get back to the house while he was out.

75

The window of his study is usually open, and that's the way I got in before. I looked in the window, and there I saw the young lady, Miss Mandle. She was lying down on the sofa, with a rug over her, reading a book. Well, thinks I, this is not the way I'm going to get in tonight. I'll have to sleep in the tool-shed.

"I was looking in the window when I heard a shot. The young lady didn't seem to hear it, because she didn't look up from her book. I couldn't understand it. Poachers don't go shooting on common-land, especially at this time of the year, and I wondered what could have happened. I knew Mr Jetheroe had not returned, because I should have seen him come up the garden path from the tool-house.

"Thinks I, there's something fishy about this, and I'm going to watch. So I got into the laurel bushes near the front door and waited. I was there about a quarter of an hour when I heard his footsteps coming up the drive. It's a gravel drive, and you can hear it plain. When I saw him I was so surprised that you could have knocked me down with a feather. His face was white, as white as a sheet, and he was talking and muttering to himself."

"How could you see his face in the dark?" asked Socrates.

"There's a fanlight over the door, sir, and there was a light in the hall," said Mr Gritt triumphantly, "that's how I saw!"

"Could you hear anything he muttered?"

Gritt nodded.

"I heard him say: 'At last, at last, I've got you,' and something about 'swinging.' As he stood on the doorstep I saw him take something out of his pocket and look at it. It was a revolver. He looked at it for a long time, then slipped it into his pocket. Then he hesitated a bit and took it out again, and he sort of broke it in two – you know how you break revolvers, like you break guns when you want to load them. He was muttering, but I couldn't hear what he said, and he put the pistol back in his pocket, opened the door and went in."

Bob Stone's eyes were on the other's face.

"Well," he breathed, "what do you think now?"

"All right, Mr Gritt," said Socrates; "will you wait outside, and when I've turned the matter over in my mind, I'll call you in."

Mr Gritt staggered out, and they heard his halting steps pass along the passage into the street.

"You've got him, you've got him, Soc!" said Bob Stone.

"Got him?" repeated Socrates with a little smile. "How the devil have I got him?"

"He was obviously the murderer."

Socrates shook his head.

"The only thing that is obvious," he said, "is that he saw the murder – "

"But the revolver?"

"The revolver was an ordinary revolver. You heard Gritt say how he broke it in the middle, and – "

"Well," said the other impatiently, "couldn't he kill a man with a revolver?"

Socrates nodded.

"He could," he said, "but John Mandle was killed with a 35 automatic pistol which does not break in the middle. As for Jetheroe – " Socrates rose. "I shall seize the first opportunity, which will be tonight, to call upon that gentleman and discover from him just what he saw, and what he heard, at the Three Oaks on the night John Mandle met his death."

A SHOT IN THE DARK

There is at Scotland Yard a man who lives wholly in the past. He dwells amidst musty newspaper files and finds his joy in the recalling of forgotten cases. He can recite in detail every incident, every scrap of evidence in trials, generations old. To him, that afternoon, Socrates wrote a long and confidential letter, and dispatched it by express post. Molly and his brother had returned from their visit to Jetheroe by the time he had finished, and were apparently so absorbed in one another's society that Bob Stone went home in disgust.

A further diversion came in the shape of Mandle's solicitor, who arrived that afternoon and interviewed the girl. To her amazement she discovered that John Mandle had left the bulk of his property to her. The will was a very old one, made the year of his marriage to her mother, who was the sole legatee. Mandle must have overlooked the fact that in these circumstances the property would pass to his step-daughter; for he had made no codicil.

It was bewildering news, for John Mandle had died a rich man. Privately the solicitor informed Socrates that he had had many talks with Mandle, who had certainly no intention of benefiting Molly by his death.

"I don't know what he intended doing with his property," said the lawyer, "but like so many other men, he put off making his final dispositions. Miss Templeton is touched by what she thinks is her stepfather's generosity, and I have not attempted to undeceive her. I should imagine that nothing was further from his thoughts or his desire than that she should inherit his estate."

Socrates nodded.

"I don't think we can do any good by telling her what John's intentions were," he said, and there the matter ended, and to the end of her life the girl believed that her fortune was intentionally bequeathed by the man who hated her, not because she had injured him, but because she was a living reminder of his treachery to her mother.

For John Mandle had practised the most heartless of deceptions, had produced forged death certificates to account for the mysterious absence of her mother's husband, and had persuaded her all un-wittingly into a bigamous marriage.

The lawyer stayed to dinner, and his presence extended the meal so that it was nearly nine o'clock when he rose to catch his train back to London.

"It's too late to see Jetheroe tonight," said Socrates.

"Were you going to see him?" asked Lexington in surprise.

"Yes. What did you think of him?"

Lexington hesitated.

"I don't know. He's rather decent I thought." They were smoking their cigars, pacing the road outside the inn, when Lexington remembered.

"There was a parcel came up for you from Haslemere. It looks like a rather fat book."

"Oh, yes," said Socrates checking in his stride, "where is it?"

"I told them to put it in the sitting-room." Socrates went quickly into the room and found the parcel on the sideboard. The girl was reading preparatory to going to bed.

"I was wondering what that was," she smiled as he tore off the wrappings. "My, what a big book!"

"It's the best gazetteer of England I know," said Socrates and turned the leaves.

"Are you looking for some place?" she said, rising and putting down her own book with a stifled yawn.

"I'm looking for Poppyland which all good children visit about nine p.m. I think you had better go to bed, young lady."

"And I'm for once in complete agreement with you, Mr Smith."

"One of these days you'll call me Soc," he said under his breath, but she heard him.

"Why?" she asked.

"Do you know why, Lexington?"

Lex was staring at his seemingly unconscious brother.

"Take no notice of old Soc, Molly," he said, "I'll walk with you to the foot of the stairs."

"I wonder what would happen to her if you didn't," said Socrates innocently, but they had gone out and the door had closed with a bang behind them.

Lexington came back in a quarter of an hour.

"We had a turn up and down the road," he said unconcernedly.

"I guessed you would."

Socrates did not raise his eyes from his book.

The two keys he had taken from the burnt desk lay on the table.

"Pool-in-the-what?" he said stabbing the burnt label with his finger.

"Is it the name of a village?"

Socrates shook his head.

"I hoped it was," he said. "Of course there are places like Slowe-in-the-Wold and Widdicome-in-the-Moor and a few other places in the Weald, but there's no Pool in the Weald, or the Moor, or the Wold. So it must be a farm, and the only place where the farms have such picturesque names is Devonshire. So I guess it is Pool-in-the-Moor."

He shut the book with a bang.

"Why are you so eager to know?"

"Why was John Mandle so anxious to keep the place a secret?" asked Socrates. "So anxious that he kept the keys in the most secretive recess of his desk?"

"What are you going to do?"

"I am wiring tomorrow to the biggest land agent in Devonshire to ask him if he can locate Pool-in-the-Moor. If I fail there I shall try the Weald in Sussex, and as a last resort, I'll try the Fen country. It may

THE THREE OAK MYSTERY

after all be Pool-in-the-Marsh. Why these people do not call their farms by Christian names I do not know. And now," pocketing the keys, "may I ask you to take a turn up the road with me? I admit," said Socrates modestly, "that I am not beautiful and that my hand, which you seldom hold, is rough and horny."

"I don't hold anybody's hand," said Lexington loudly; "now just you drop it, Soc! You're annoying me."

"Come on, Lothario," said Soc, seizing his cap. "We'll walk up to the burnt mansion and see if we can get an inspiration."

They stepped out briskly along the dark road. The rain had ceased, and in the moonlight white rays of smoke were still rising from the ruined "Woodlands." Only the bulk of the summer house stood whole and lonely amidst the desolation.

"Do you seriously think that Jetheroe knows anything about this murder?" asked Lexington.

"I'm certain," was the unexpected reply, unexpected because up till then Lexington did not know of the charge laid by Mr Gritt, nor the information he had conveyed, in his malice.

The gist of this Socrates briefly related.

"I am certain that Jetheroe witnessed the murder," said Socrates, "and the little talk I had with Molly just before dinner supports in every point the story Gritt told. Jetheroe did go out to look for the man who had frightened her, and she was lying on the sofa reading and the window was open and she even heard Gritt's footsteps on the path."

"She didn't hear the shot though?"

"No, that's understandable. The window faces north, the sound came from the south, or rather the south-east. Moreover – "

The men stopped in their tracks.

It was the sound of a shot, startlingly distinct in the still night air, that had arrested them. The explosion seemed near at hand.

"What was that?" asked Lexington, his heart beating a little quicker. "It was a revolver shot!"

"No, it was a shot from an automatic pistol; you could tell that by the repercussion," said Socrates quietly, "and it came from the direction of the Three Oaks."

He took a small hand-torch from his pocket and threw a beam along the hedgerow.

"Here is the path," he said. "Now, steady the Buffs, Lexington! And whatever else you do, keep out of my line of fire!"

In his right hand had appeared, as if by magic, a fat ugly weapon with a short barrel and an unhealthy calibre. He ran lightly down the twisting path, checking his speed and extinguishing his light before they came to the avenue through the bushes.

He halted for a second as they came in sight of the great branch visible against the background of velvet sky. There was no sound but their own breathing and he went on, flashing his lamp on the ground before him.

"Oh, yes!" he said suddenly.

It was the same "Oh, yes" he had used before, and the same provocation was there. A man lay on his face beneath the branch, his arms extended motionless.

A trickle of blood was running from under his head.

"Jetheroe!" cried Socrates Smith, and was stooping to turn the body on its back.

And then from near at hand came a peal of maniacal laughter, a shrill "Hoo-Hoo!" of delight that chilled the blood of the young man. Swiftly Socrates turned his light in the direction, but no one was visible.

"Come out or I'll shoot," he said.

"*Ping!*"

The bullet missed him by the fraction of an inch, but he had seen the flash and twice his heavy revolver barked, and then there was a rustle of bushes and silence.

The two men dashed into the bush and heard the rustle of branches as their quarry fled.

It was a quarter of an hour before they gave up their search and returned to the Three Oaks. And here the surprise of the evening awaited them.

The body of Theodore Kenneth Ward, alias Jetheroe, had vanished!

THE DIARY

"Thank God she doesn't know it's her father," said Socrates, after a particularly painful interview with the girl, "and yet I guess that she had a feeling that there was something more than friendship in that man's attitude."

"Stone won't tell her, will he?" asked Lexington.

Socrates shook his head.

"Stone's too dead beat to tell anybody anything," he said. "He heard the shot and turned out all his servants to search for the lunatic."

"Can Jetheroe's people throw any light on the mystery?"

Socrates shook his head.

"He was in his library, that's all they knew, and he left it without any word and went out. That's the last they saw of him."

"Was his window open?"

"Yes, his window was open, as Gritt said it was."

"Is it possible somebody communicated with him through the window," said Lexington, "and persuaded him to come out?"

"That is not only possible, it is a certainty. Jetheroe was lured to his fate, and went expecting it. We found his revolver with the hammer raised, loaded in six chambers. He must have come with his gun in hand to an appointment which has likely enough ended in his death."

"But where is the body?" asked Lex. "We've searched the valley all night, and we've found no trace of it. The only thing we know is that Jetheroe has disappeared."

Socrates Smith had asked himself the same question many times.

"He must have confederates – I'm talking about the murderer," he said. "And that upsets all my theories. Yet I cannot exclude the possibility of other people being in these crimes. Let me see!" He stretched back in his chair and ticked off the incidents, finger by finger.

"He killed Mandle. He made elaborate preparations to kill Bob Stone. He has probably killed Jetheroe; now who else is he going to kill?"

Lexington shifted uneasily in his chair.

"It gives me the creeps, Soc," he said, "another half an inch and you'd have got yours last night."

Soc nodded.

"The question is," he said softly and meditatively, "is it necessary that Molly should die? I don't think so."

"Good God!" gasped Lexington springing up, his face drawn. "You don't suggest in that cold-blooded fashion that they have any grudge against Molly?"

"I wouldn't rule out even that possibility," said Soc thoughtfully. "It depends entirely upon – " he stopped.

"You've a disgusting habit of cutting your sentences short," said Lex irritably. "What does it depend on?"

"I've only a theory so far," said Soc, but in this matter he was not telling the truth, for his theory was a certainty in his mind, only – there remained Pool-in-the-Moor to be cleared up, and that it was Pool-in-the-Moor he discovered in the course of the day.

"An untenanted farmhouse three miles out of Ashburton on the Newton Abbot road," was the message he received from Exeter. "The proprietor is a Frenchman, who never visits his property. It was purchased by him twenty years ago for £630 from Haggit & George of Torquay."

"That is what I call a business-like communication," said Socrates with satisfaction. "What is happening, Lex?" he asked. "I heard a babble of talk downstairs."

"They've arrested Gritt," said Lexington; "our inspector friend is determined to arrest somebody, and Gritt has been breathing fire and torture against Jetheroe and uttering mysterious threats of what he was going to do to him."

Socrates nodded.

"That is fairly easily explained," he said. "He thought he was going to get Jetheroe arrested. Poor devil! I wish he had been now. If I'd followed the advice of Bob Stone, Jetheroe would have been alive and well today."

The young man had some other trouble on his mind than the woes of Mr Gritt, or even the tragic fate which had overtaken Jetheroe.

"Do you seriously think, Soc, that Molly is in any kind of danger, from any cause whatsoever?"

His brother shook his head.

"Honestly I can't tell you definitely," he said. "In certain eventualities, there is a danger. Will you answer a question if I put it to you straightly, Lex?"

"Yes," said the other quietly.

"Are you in love with Molly Templeton?"

Lex hesitated and then: "Yes I am," he said in the same tone. "I love her very dearly."

"Have you told her so?"

"No, I haven't," Lex shook his head. "I haven't had the courage to risk a refusal."

"Are you going to tell her so?" persisted Socrates.

"I will at the first opportunity. It would be indecent to talk of love at a moment like this when the poor girl is simply distracted by the disappearance of her best friend."

Again Socrates nodded.

"I see the position," said he. "What do you think she feels towards you?"

"I think she likes me."

"Loves you?"

"Well, I couldn't say that without being a conceited pup," said Lexington, "but I think she likes me very much. I think she knows that I love her."

"That's all it is necessary to know," said Socrates. "If a woman knows a man loves her and continues to treat him like a human being, you may be sure she loves him."

"Do you think so?" he asked eagerly.

"I'm not out giving advice on how to tell when a lady loves you," said Socrates with a half smile, though he was serious enough. "Let me know how this thing progresses, will you? You see, Lex" — he squeezed the boy's arm affectionately — "you're the beginning and end of my family, and I'm rather interested in your affairs, particularly an affair which may — " again he stopped, an irritating practice of his.

"May what?" asked Lexington patiently.

"May upset my household arrangements," said Soc, but the other knew that that was not what he was going to say. And then a suspicion dawned on him.

"You don't think Molly knows anything about these horrible crimes, do you, Soc?"

"No, I don't," said the other, but he hesitated just a little too long, and Lexington misconstrued that pause.

"Do you think she knows — " he began in horrified tones, and Soc laughed aloud.

"Go and make love to her, my boy, and leave me alone," he said. "Would you like to go to a nice healthy inquest this afternoon, or am I going solo?"

"So far as I'm concerned you're going solo," said Lexington, and then: "I suppose there's no chance of your being shot at on the way?"

"Very little chance. I am taking Bob for a bodyguard. You can pursue your philandering with a clear conscience."

The inquest was a formal affair and was adjourned as Socrates expected it to be. The new development represented by the disappearance of Jetheroe gave the murder a peculiarly sinister aspect, and Scotland Yard was represented at the trial by one of its highest officials.

"I don't think we can do better than leave you in charge, Mr Smith," he said when the proceedings were over. "As a matter of form we shall have to send a man down to take official control, and he will probably get all the kudos that is going."

"He can have a few of the bullets that are going too," said Socrates, and told what he had no occasion to tell at the inquest, the story of the shot in the dark.

"Do you think it is the act of a madman?"

"It is possible," replied Socrates. "On the other hand, that maniacal laughter may have been part of the general scheme of camouflage. Remember this, that the fight is between the nerve of the murderer and the nerve of the man who is trying to get him. And the nerve that breaks first is the nerve that loses. A good creepy burst of wild and fiendish merriment is calculated to shake the nerve of better men than I, and incidentally spoil his good shooting. Unhappily for the murderer, my nerves remained at concert pitch," he said.

"You're a wonderful fellow, Mr Smith. It's a thousand pities you did not remain in the force."

"If I had remained in the force I should have been a perfectly useless commissioner by now," said Socrates Smith, and hastily apologized, for his companion held that exalted rank.

"There are many things I cannot understand about Mandle's death," said the commissioner at parting. "Why were handcuffs in his pocket? Whom did he expect to arrest?"

The discovery of the handcuffs had been made when the body was searched at Haslemere. Curiously enough, Socrates had not made a search.

"Heaven knows," was his reply.

They talked of the fire and of the losses which had been sustained by members of the house party.

"I only brought one suitcase. I shall miss that old fellow," said Socrates. "Miss Templeton lost practically everything except her diary, which I gather she keeps under her pillow. Girl-like it is probably filled with her most sacred thoughts."

The commissioner laughed.

Recounting the conversation after Bob had gone home – he had never attempted to spend an evening with them since the night of the fire – Socrates bantered the girl.

"I didn't see any diary," said Lexington in surprise, and Socrates chuckled.

"Mr Smith, I think you were a pig to tell the commissioner that," said the crimson-faced girl. "I don't put sacred thoughts in my diary at all. Anyway I don't have many."

His twinkling eyes were fixed on hers.

"When I see a young lady hugging a fat little volume that is locked," he said solemnly, "I scent an outpouring of soul, a self-communing which is very refreshing to an ancient like myself."

She pleaded guilty. She had kept diaries for years, she said, but they had all been destroyed in the fire except the one which she had mechanically grasped when she was aroused by the smoke and the crackling of the burning building.

"Why did you rag Molly about her diary?" asked Lexington when they were alone.

"Why shouldn't I rag anybody about anything?" asked Socrates.

"Do you think there's anything in that diary – " he did not complete the sentence.

"Yes?" encouraged the other.

"About Mandle or Jetheroe? Anything that is dangerous to her?"

"It is very possible," replied Socrates, so seriously that his brother's jaw dropped.

"But she knows nothing about them that she hasn't told us, Soc."

"I merely say it is very possible," said Socrates, and took up his newspaper.

Lexington sought out the girl and took her for a walk. It had become a practice of theirs, this little stroll in front of the hotel, and every time he had accompanied her the walk had grown a longer one.

"You don't mind my brother fooling, do you?" he asked.

"I think he is a dear," she replied.

"Oh," he said in surprise, "I thought you didn't like him?"

She laughed softly.

"How can you tell whether I like people or not?" she asked, a fatal question.

"How do I know that you like me?" he asked, huskily bold.

"You?" she said, and if she was not surprised, her tone was perfectly feigned. "Why, of course you know I like you, Lexington."

"And I like you," said Lex lamely, and then before he knew what had happened, or understood the impulse which moved him, she was in his arms and her lips were against his. It was a tremendous and awful moment for Lexington Smith. He could stand outside of himself and be amazed at his own audacity. Something like a panic seized him and he had an insane desire to run away, but he held tightly to the girl and, if the truth be told, he might have found some difficulty in disengaging himself from the arms which had stolen timidly round his neck.

"And there let us leave them, gentle reader," quoth Socrates Smith, an unwilling but nevertheless interested spectator, since they had chosen for that occasion the crest of a gentle rise so that they stood outlined against the deep orange of the western sky.

It was an hour later before he heard their voices outside of the sitting-room door, and then Lexington came in alone, flushed, triumphant, walking on air.

He shut the door behind him and sat at the table confronting his brother with shining eyes.

"Soc, old bird, I have something to tell you," he said.

"You're engaged to Molly Templeton," said Soc, and Lex gasped.

"How did you know?" he demanded.

"I saw you," was the calm reply. "A beautiful sight that recalled to me my lost opportunities."

"You saw me?" gasped Lex incredulously.

"You chose the crest of the rise for your tender embrace," said Socrates. "I thought you did it on purpose," he added innocently, and Lex's face was the colour of a beetroot.

"If Molly only knew, she'd – " he began hollowly.

"Molly doesn't know, and besides it's not an unusual phenomenon in these parts," said Socrates, and he was very thoughtful.

"Are you keeping your engagement a secret?"

"Did you hear us as well?" asked Lex suspiciously.

"No, I was wondering. Are you?"

"Yes," nodded Lexington. "Molly thinks that it would not be decent to announce the fact so soon after Mr Mandle's death."

Soc nodded, pulling slowly at his cigar.

"I am very glad," he said. "We're moving to Prince's Place tomorrow. Bob insists upon our staying there, and it would hardly be nice for poor old Bob – "

"Can't we stay on here?" asked Lexington with a frown.

The other shook his head.

"We shall have to remain here in the neighbourhood until the inquest is cleared up, and it would be ungracious to refuse Bob's invitation," he said. "I'm afraid you'll have to stick it for that time, Lex. There is no reason why you shouldn't be married just as soon as you like after we get back to London."

"Does Molly know we are going to Prince's Place?"

Soc nodded.

"She didn't tell me," complained the young man.

"She probably didn't attach the same importance to the move as you do," smiled Socrates. "Anyway, you won't be dull, Lex. It is a beautiful spot with a wonderful garden. And I can't see how we can get out of going anyway."

"I suppose not," replied Lexington dubiously.

As he passed the girl's room that night on his way to his room he slipped an unnecessarily long letter he had written to her under the door. There was no reason in the world why he should assure her of his love, which could hardly have cooled in so short a time, but in the chronology of lovers, minutes of partings are accounted centuries, and centuries, in one another's associations, flash past as seconds.

The girl interrupted the writing up of her diary, that precious diary she had retrieved from the fire, to pick up the letter and read it. It was an ecstatic letter, and she sat with her face aglow, taking in every scrawled word, merciful to the involved composition. And in the end, she folded it carefully and put it under her pillow, and added yet another closely written paragraph to the recorded events of the day.

She went to bed, but not immediately to sleep. She was dozing when a distant clock struck one, and fell into an uneasy sleep soon afterwards. And then she opened her eyes. She was lying facing the wall and she had seen a flash of light travel along the wall near her head. She turned quickly in the bed and saw a dark figure standing by the writing -table and a yellow circle of light moving across its surface.

"Who is there?" she gasped.

"Don't make a sound, if you value your life!"

The voice was squeaky and high, and in the reflected gleam of the light she saw the glimpse of blue steel.

"What do you want?" she asked in a terrified whisper, but the figure made no answer.

She could only glimpse the face, which was half covered by a blue silk handkerchief. The rest was hidden by the peak of a golf cap pulled down over the forehead.

Presently, with a little exclamation, the searcher found that which he was seeking. She saw him slip something into his pocket and take up the pistol which she had glimpsed from the table. The light he carried went out suddenly and he backed to the door.

"Don't scream. I'll be standing outside for ten minutes," he said. "If you make a noise – "

He did not complete the sentence, but the menace of it struck cold into the girl's heart.

The door closed softly behind him. How had be got in? She remembered that she had locked the door. She listened and heard the stairs creak. Minutes seemed interminable. At last she could stand it no longer and springing out of bed, she seized her dressing-gown and flung open the door. She knew Socrates' room was next to her own and she knocked at the panel and his voice immediately answered: "Who is that?"

"It's Molly," she said tearfully, and she heard a word of surprise and the light went up.

"What is the matter?" he asked, and she gasped her story, hysterically.

He picked up a pistol by the side of his bed and ran out of the room and down the stairs. He returned in five minutes with the news that the front door of the inn was unbarred and open, but that there was nobody in sight.

"Now let's have a look at your room," he said, and turned his flashlight on the outside of the door.

The end of the key was protruding and he nodded.

"That's how he came in," he said. "These old-fashioned keys are pretty easy to turn if you have a strong enough pair of nippers. Have you lost anything?"

"I don't know," she said. "He was making a search. I was wondering whether I had any letters of Mr Mandle's."

"Was there anything on the table?"

"No," she said, and then with an exclamation, "my diary!"

"Your diary?" he said quickly.

"It was there," she pointed and went red and white, "and it's gone!"

DON'T LEAVE MOLLY

"There are half a dozen ways a man can get into the Chequers," reported Socrates when he came in to breakfast, "and I'm jolly glad we're going to Prince's Place today. This is certainly not an impregnable fortress."

"I wish to heaven you'd called me, Soc," said Lexington reproachfully.

"I managed to calm Miss Templeton without assistance," replied Soc, "and I really don't know what other service you could have rendered — do you, Molly?"

She shook her head, not raising her eyes from her plate.

"But why the dickens did they want your diary, Molly?" asked Lex in a troubled voice. "Was there something in it of great importance?"

"There was a lot in it of great importance," she said vigorously, "of great importance to me. Oh, Mr Smith, I could die of shame when I think of that diary in somebody else's hands."

She was so obviously distressed that Socrates did not attempt to be humorous, and indeed he was not in a humorous mood.

"Were there any entries concerning Mr Mandle?" he asked.

She nodded.

"Yes, there were several. I used to write quite a lot about him before — before — a long time ago," she corrected herself hurriedly, "and much more about Mr Jetheroe. We were such very good friends, and he was so romantic a figure that I wrote quite a lot about him."

"You can't recall what you wrote?"

She shook her head.

"No, I can't," she said. "I remember," she went on slowly, "that I wrote pages and pages about Mr Mandle's habits. Life was so dull that I took to studying him and putting my observations into writing. You see, it wasn't an ordinary day-to-day diary. And this year, if I hadn't filled up with little sketches of people, there would have been nothing to write about. I used to note how he spent the day and how he would be for hours in his summer house when he wasn't in the study. There's a big marble table in the summer house, and on warm days he'd take all his writing material there and stay there until sunset. Timms used to carry his lunch out to him and be on hand if he wanted anything. Mr Mandle had an electric bell fixed in the summer house that communicated with the kitchen."

Socrates nodded.

"I've seen that," he said.

"He used to sit there for hours at a time. There was a marble chair that he bought in London and of which he was very fond. They say it was a genuine antique and had come from Italy. Timms used to fill it with cushions for him, and I remember the impression I once had of him as a king enthroned – it was very much like a throne. But really I wrote nothing about him in the diary which any servant in the house could not have told the person who stole the book."

"It's queer," said Socrates quietly.

Without a word he left them alone and went up to the ruined "Woodlands," which now consisted of two blackened walls and a tangle of burnt timber. The summer house lay at the highest point of the garden and overlooked the Godalming road. It was built of white stone and was an elaborate and beautiful little building surmounted by a gilded roof. Sliding windows were fitted to its four sides, and the interior was waterproof and comfortable. What Molly had described as a throne had certainly that appearance. It was a handsome high-backed seat set behind a table of the same material.

The seat was supported on what appeared to be a solid block of marble, and there was a chaste dignity about the interior which was very impressive.

Socrates had given the summer house a casual search before, but had not attached any particular significance to John Mandle's frequent visits. After all, it was a place where a man of leisure would wish to spend his solitary hours. The view through the doorway was gorgeous, the situation in every other respect was perfect.

When he got back to the inn the two young people were still talking over the breakfast table, and as he opened the door there was a stir and a shuffling of chairs which amused him.

"I think we ought to pack," he said. "Bob is sending his car over at eleven o'clock."

He saw the shadow on the girl's face.

"Don't you like the idea of staying at Prince's Place, Molly?" he asked.

"Not very much," she admitted. "I'm very fond of Mr Stone, he's a dear man, but just now," she looked at Lex, "I don't really feel that I want to be under his roof."

Soc understood something of the girl's reluctance, but there were many reasons why the arrangement suggested by Bob Stone would be to his advantage. He wanted the privacy of a house where his comings and goings would not be observed and where he had a freer use of a telephone. Moreover Bob could offer him resources which the village did not hold. Stone maintained a large household and had two cars which might be very useful indeed.

Bob came in one of them at eleven o'clock, and was greatly concerned to learn of the girl's night adventure.

"The sooner you're at Prince's Place the better," he said irritably. "Now then, Timms, hurry up with these bags."

The girl had retained the services of all her stepfather's household, and the fact that Bob had extended his invitation to these stranded people had a lot to do with her acceptance of his offer.

Timms carried down the bags and they were packed into the limousine, Molly and Lex having already walked on ahead, for the distance was less than half a mile.

Bob looked after them with a troubled face, and Socrates, watching him, felt a momentary twinge of pity. Bob's glumness, however, wore off almost immediately.

"We'll walk too, Soc," he said. "There is no news of Jetheroe?"

Socrates shook his head.

"I don't fancy we're going to have news of him," he said. "I can't understand how they got him away."

"He may have walked," suggested Bob.

"He may have done," agreed Socrates Smith, "but the first impression I had of him was that he was pretty dangerously wounded, if he was not dead."

"And yet no trace of blood has been found, although we made a very careful examination of the path," said Bob. "If he had only been stunned and recovered, why should he not go back to his own house?"

"That is a question which I find pretty difficult to answer," replied Socrates. "In many ways Jetheroe's disappearance is much more mysterious than Mandle's murder, or the fire, or that extraordinary visitation to Molly last night."

They took the Three Oaks path, and as if by mutual agreement, they came to a stop beneath the fatal bough.

"Have you ever tried to reconstruct the crime?" asked Bob Stone.

Socrates shook his head.

"Not since the first night," he said. "I know, of course, that Mandle climbed the tree himself—"

"Climbed the tree himself with his knees in that condition?"

"I don't know anything about his knees," replied Socrates quietly. "All I know is that he climbed the tree. The first thing I looked at when I went up after him was his boots. They were heavily nailed, and there were bits of bark caught up between the nails and the sole. I have since made a microscopic examination of the bark, and there is no doubt whatever that it is the bark of an oak tree."

"How came the rope round his body?"

Socrates shook his head.

"You might just as well ask me how Jetheroe came to be in possession of John Mandle's revolver."

Bob Stone looked at the other in amazement.

"His revolver?" he said incredulously, and Soc Smith nodded.

"You know Jetheroe's pistol was found by the side of the path? The hammer was raised, suggesting that he came to an appointment, rather suspicious of the good faith of the gentleman who invited him. That revolver has been identified by Timms as one which he had seen in Mr Mandle's room; we have been able to get into touch with the gunsmith who sold him the weapon, and there is no doubt at all that it belonged to Mandle. My own theory is that Jetheroe found the revolver on the night of the murder. Possibly it had dropped from Mandle's pocket. You remember Gritt's statement, how Jetheroe came back to his house and stood muttering on the doorstep looking at a revolver which he took from his pocket. He looked at it twice, you will recall."

Stone nodded.

"That is so," he said thoughtfully; "of course he looked at it twice because it was something new to him, something which had come recently into his possession."

"Exactly," said Socrates Smith. "Though I haven't reconstructed the crime, I found the path by which our gentleman of the maniacal laughter made his escape. It's very easily followed in the daylight, and leads back to the road. If instead of dashing like a lunatic after this person I had sent Lex up to the road he should have seen him emerging from the bushes."

Stone sighed and resumed the walk.

"It's a queer case altogether," he said. "Damned queer."

Their way led them past the open gates of the White House, and Socrates glanced up the drive out of the tail of his eye, and stopping, walked back.

"What is it?" asked Bob joining him.

A stout woman was running down the drive waving her hand in frantic signal.

"I rather fancy that is Jetheroe's housekeeper," said Soc.

The woman was moist and breathless.

"I saw you gentlemen from the window," she said, "and tried to attract your attention."

"What is it?" asked Socrates quickly, "has Mr Jetheroe been found?"

"No, sir, but I've been going through the house carefully and I've found one or two strange things that I'd like you to see. You are the gentleman in charge of the case, aren't you?"

Socrates nodded, and followed the breathless lady up the drive.

"We've been so upset," she said, "that we haven't known whether we're on our heads or on our heels. I told Thomas — that's Mr Jetheroe's man — that I was certain he wasn't dead."

"Have you heard from him?" asked Socrates.

She shook her head.

"No, sir, I've not heard from him, but I'm sure it won't be long before we do."

She was evidently determined upon having her own mystery, and Socrates did not press her for further information, until she revealed the evidence which she had apparently unearthed.

She led them up the stairs, and opened the door of the bathroom with something of a dramatic flourish.

"This is what I found," she said.

On a chair were two or three handkerchiefs, though it was difficult at first to recognize them as such, for they were stiff and caked with some dark brown stain.

"Blood!" said Socrates. "Where did you find them?"

"Under the bath tub," said the woman. "I was having a turn out this morning and I found them pushed right under. I know they weren't there a week ago, because I had this room cleaned under my own eye. Mr Jetheroe was rather particular."

"Those are bloodstains all right," said Bob Stone, taking one of the stained squares from the other's hand.

"And that isn't all I found," said the woman triumphantly. "I put two and two together and I looked round and remembered that Mr Jetheroe kept his medicine chest in here. Not exactly a medicine chest, but a cupboard. Most people keep their medicines in the bathroom," she explained, "and Mr Jetheroe had a sort of first-aid locker here."

"Is that it?" asked Bob, pointing to a white cupboard which hung on the wall.

"I've never thought to look before," she said, opening the two doors and revealing an array of bottles and a confusion of bandages and lint which were entangled in a heap in one corner. "Somebody's been here since I saw it last," she said; "Mr Jetheroe was very neat and tidy – and besides, look at that!" – she pointed to a bloody thumb-print on the shelf.

Socrates took out the bandages carefully. Two or three had little brown stains, a bottle half-filled with iodine stood corkless on a lower shelf. It had been used by somebody who had handled it carelessly, as a brown rim of the fluid testified.

"After I found this," said Mrs Howard importantly, "I looked carefully round, especially the bath. If you look, sir, you can see that somebody has been using the bathroom tap to bathe a wound."

There was a tiny speckle of stain on the smooth white side of the bath to support her hypothesis. Socrates nodded.

"You ought to be a detective, Mrs Howard," he said good-humouredly. "There's no doubt about that, Bob, is there?"

He pointed to the bath. Bob nodded.

"He evidently got in here and cleaned himself up. He used a bandage and probably one of these linen pads," he went on, taking from the cupboard a handful of small antiseptic pads which the careful householder keeps against moments of emergency.

"But why didn't he stay?" asked Socrates puzzled. "What reason had he for disappearing? When do you think Mr Jetheroe came?" he asked.

"Last night?"

The woman hesitated.

"He may have done, sir, he may have come in the night before. You see we weren't expecting anything unusual, and nobody stayed up. Mr Jetheroe always used his key. Until we were wakened by the police at three o'clock in the morning we had no idea that anything had happened to him."

"I see," said Socrates. "Then there is a possibility that between the hour of his shooting and the time you were awakened he may have come in, dressed his wounds and cleared out again. It certainly looks so."

He examined the cupboard again and made a more careful inspection of the bathroom.

"May I see Mr Jetheroe's own bedroom?" he asked.

"That's what I was going to suggest, sir," said the housekeeper leading the way. "I haven't been able to take stock yet, so I don't know whether any clothes have disappeared. I do remember the following morning that his collar drawer was pulled open, but apparently none of his other things were touched."

Mr Jetheroe was a methodical man and a neat one. He was in the habit, so the housekeeper told Socrates, of valeting himself and putting away his own clothing. Three or four suits were hanging in a deep cupboard.

"You haven't looked at these, have you?" asked Bob.

Socrates shook his head.

"Let's have them out," he said.

The second hanger that was unhooked from its suspending rail removed any doubt he might have had as to the fate which had overtaken Jetheroe. It was a dark shooting-coat, and the shoulders were suspiciously immobile. Socrates carried the coat to the light.

"This is the coat he was wearing when he was attacked," he said. "Look, the shoulders are stiff with blood. Well, that settles Mr Jetheroe. He's alive."

"But where?" asked Bob.

Socrates shrugged.

"You might as well ask me, but why? He has his own reason for disappearing, and I daresay we shall know all about it in a day or two. Thank you, Mrs Howard," he turned to the woman. "You certainly have the detective's instinct, and you can relieve your mind of any worry you may have as to whether Mr Jetheroe is alive or dead."

A quarter of an hour later he was walking down the beautiful drive that led to Prince's Place. From the moment they left the house until their arrival at Bob's residence neither man had spoken, and it was Socrates who broke the silence.

"This discovery," he said quietly, "has relieved me of a great deal of personal anxiety."

"What do you mean?" asked the other in surprise. "Were you very much worried about Jetheroe disappearing?"

"In a sense," said Soc, "but worried is hardly the word I should have used. I was apprehensive. Now that Jetheroe is in the land of the living I have at least a reprieve. For the unknown slayer of John Mandle will certainly devote his attention to the killing of Jetheroe before he turns his homicidal eye upon me."

Bob looked at him open-eyed.

"Do you think that you are in any danger?" he asked slowly.

"I am pretty certain about that," replied Socrates, "and I should imagine that the method of my destruction is going to be a peculiarly sticky one – both for me and my murderer," he added grimly.

Lex and the girl did not arrive till some time afterwards.

Bob Stone had given her the best room in the house, and when she had inspected her new habitation she was filled with praise of Bob and his thoughtfulness. It was a large room overlooking an old-world garden, a garden which had existed and had lifted its fragrance to the clear heavens even in the days when beribboned cavaliers had lorded it at the old Chequers. It had been an ancient garden when Nelson bowled down the Portsmouth Road on his way to join the *Victory*. It had seen successions of edifices known as "Prince's Place" rise and crumble, and was today as fresh, as beautiful, and as comforting, as it had been when its Elizabethan gardeners had laid down its quaint beds.

Molly was overjoyed at the news; she was happy but bewildered.

"I cannot understand why he should have gone away," she said, puzzled. "He's the most matter-of-fact man, and really, in spite of his picturesque appearance, there is nothing whatever mysterious about him. Do you think that he is in the neighbourhood?"

"I don't think so," replied Socrates. They were walking in the garden after lunch.

"But why should he hide at all?" insisted the girl with a little frown. "I don't understand it. Mr Jetheroe has done nothing wrong, has he?" she asked quickly.

"He has done nothing wrong recently," said Socrates, and she looked at him doubtfully.

"Recently?" she repeated.

"Mr Jetheroe has had a very hard life," Socrates hastened to explain his ambiguous words, remembering that the time might come when the girl's relationship with Jetheroe would be revealed. "And, my dear, you have to remember that scientists tell us that all our cell structures change every seven years, so that the present Mr Jetheroe can hardly be saddled with the indiscretions of his youth. I repeat he has had a very hard life and has suffered unjustly at somebody's hands."

"Do you think he was concerned in the murder of Mr Mandle?" she asked, turning pale.

He shook his head.

"There is no question in my mind that he is perfectly innocent of that murder. But – "

"But?" she repeated.

"But there is a little mystery about him which has to be cleared up."

"But why is he hiding?" she repeated. "Why should he hide? What has he to fear?"

"He has to fear a repetition of his unpleasant experience of the night before last," said Soc gravely, "and now don't puzzle your pretty little head about these things. There is Lexington, who I have no doubt can tell you something ever so much more interesting than I can invent."

He was called from the couple a few minutes later. A telephone message had come from London, and he hastened to the instrument to learn that a messenger was on his way to Prince's Place with an important communication. The messenger proved to be a young man from the London and Surrey Bank.

"Our general manager sent me down. We communicated with Scotland Yard and I was instructed to come to you," said the visitor.

"What is it?" asked Socrates.

"I'm at the Lothbury branch of the London and Surrey Bank," explained the clerk, "and we carry Mr Jetheroe's account – "

"Just one moment."

He had taken the visitor into the dining-room.

"I think if you don't mind we'll walk out into the garden," he said, "into the cabbage garden for preference," he added humorously, "because although cabbages have hearts they have no ears, and this house is full of strange servants. Now," he demanded when they were alone, save for the harmless vegetables he had described, "you say Mr Jetheroe's account was at the Lothbury branch of the London and Surrey Bank. Well?"

"Yes, sir," said the clerk, "we saw the account of Mr Jetheroe's disappearance, but apparently we saw it too late, for an hour before we had cashed a cheque for £500 on his account." He took out from his pocketbook an envelope and produced a cheque form.

Socrates examined it. It was signed in a bold hand and the signature he knew was Jetheroe's.

"Who presented this cheque?" he asked.

"Mr Jetheroe himself, according to the cashier who paid it out."

"Did the cashier notice anything peculiar about him?"

The clerk nodded.

"His head was bandaged, and the cashier asked him if he'd had an accident. Mr Jetheroe replied that he had fallen from a motorcycle, and our cashier thought it was rather remarkable that a gentleman of Mr Jetheroe's age should go in for motorcycling."

"Did he give any indication as to where he was going?"

"No, sir," replied the clerk. "All he said was that it might be necessary for him to cash further cheques, but that it was very improbable that he could come himself."

Socrates Smith scratched his ear thoughtfully.

"Is it permitted to ask how Mr Jetheroe's account stands at the bank?"

"He has a considerable balance, sir. The manager told me that in all probability I should be asked that question, and he gave me the exact figures. He has over £4,000 in cash, and a very considerable number of securities deposited with us. He inherited a lot of money from an aunt about six years ago – we used to carry her account too: that is how we came to be his bankers. We conduct his business, draw his dividends, and generally act as his agents when he is abroad. Our manager got a little bit nervous about the publicity," the clerk went on, "and he thought the best thing to do was to communicate with Scotland Yard, and, after consulting our head office, that is what he did."

"Thank you," said Socrates after a while. "I was certain that Mr Jetheroe was alive and I had proof of the fact this morning. When was this cheque cashed?"

"Yesterday morning about half past eleven, and in view of the message – "

"The message," said Socrates in surprise, "what do you mean?"

"Oh Lord!" said the embarrassed clerk, "I forgot to tell you. Look, sir," he turned the cheque over. There was a line of scrawled writing near the perforated edge. It was written in pencil and was faint.

Socrates carried the cheque to the light and read:

S S. Don't leave Molly. J

A MARBLE THRONE

It was a message intended for him. Of that there was no doubt. Jetheroe knew that the bank would immediately communicate with Scotland Yard when his disappearance was remarked upon and that the cheque would come into the hands of Socrates Smith.

"S S. Don't leave Molly. J" read Socrates again.

So the girl was in danger, and Jetheroe knew without knowing from whence or in what shape the danger would come.

"I'm very sorry, sir," stammered the clerk. "That was really what I came down about. You see the cashier didn't notice the message until the cheque was turned into the manager's office. He spotted it at once, because we make a practice at the bank when a customer draws a cheque in his own favour of getting him to endorse his name on the cheque. When the manager turned it over he found that by some mistake the cashier had paid out without this endorsement. Of course, it is not absolutely necessary, but it is a practice at the bank. It was then that he discovered the writing."

So Jetheroe was deliberately hiding himself and intended to remain in hiding. Moreover, Socrates inferred, Jetheroe would not be on hand to afford the girl the protection which he craved from the detective.

He borrowed one of Bob's cars to drive the young man back to the station and returned to Prince's Place in time for dinner.

Bob knew that he had had a visitor, but Socrates did not tell him or Lex who that visitor had been or the purport of his visit. Socrates has been described as secretive, and it was not an unfair description. His *alter ego* lived within and communed with himself.

There were very few people in the world who needed less the encouragement and help which outside consultation brings than Socrates Smith. Only, he was a little more thoughtful, a little more reticent, and a little less companionable in these moments of self-communion, and Bob Stone, who recognized the symptoms, jumped at the conclusion that it was the discovery in Mr Jetheroe's bathroom which reduced Socrates Smith to silence through the meal.

Despite his preoccupations Soc did not fail to notice with pleasant surprise that Bob Stone's attitude both toward Lex and the girl was all that could be desired. Apparently he had accepted the evidence of his eyes and knew that fate had marked these two young people for one another, and being the shrewd man he was, he had mastered his own desires and had accepted the situation philosophically.

"Well," said Bob at parting that night, "you've had quite an exciting three days."

"Three days?" said Socrates Smith in genuine surprise. "It seems like three years!"

"I have been talking to Molly tonight," said Bob, "about 'The Woodlands.' She has decided to rebuild the place and sell it. It is too full of unpleasant memories for her to live there, she says, and I agree."

Soc nodded.

"I hope they won't start rebuilding until I've had a very complete rake over," he said.

"Do you still expect to find evidence in the ruins?" asked Bob.

Socrates nodded.

"I've had three men there since the morning after the fire, and the Salvage Department in London has lent me one of their best and most knowledgeable men."

"I saw some people poking round as we went past today," said Bob. "I didn't know they were working for you. I think it's rather a forlorn hope."

"I think so too," agreed Socrates, "but as you know, it is from these forlorn hopes that one gets the best and most promising material."

The next morning, as was his usual practice, he walked over to "The Woodlands" and interviewed the salvage man, and the interview was not a very encouraging one.

"I've never seen so thorough and complete a destruction in my life," said the official, "there is hardly a scrap of woodwork that isn't burnt."

"Have you been through the remains of the desk?"

The other nodded.

"I've practically passed it through a sieve," he said, "but there was nothing there. You were up last night looking round, weren't you?"

"I?" said Socrates. "No, I didn't come near the place."

"One of our men saw somebody wandering around with an electric lamp," said the officer; "I thought it must be you."

"What time was this?"

"Some time after dark," said the salvage man. "My man lives at a cottage down the road, and he'd been to the Chequers to get a drink and was going home. It must have been half past nine, for the bar closes at that time. He saw somebody moving about, but took no particular notice, thinking it was you. When he told me this morning I thought the same."

Socrates Smith was silent. It had never occurred to him that the mystery man could expect to find anything of interest in the wreckage.

"You'd better arrange for one of your men to stay on guard tonight," he said. "And whilst I think of it, tell the workmen to be very careful not to use the summer house to take their meals in. I saw a couple of them there yesterday."

The salvage official nodded.

"I've already warned them," he said. "It's a beautiful little place."

They walked slowly up the steep path of the knoll on which the summer house was sited.

"The marble is very rare and probably very valuable," explained Socrates, and then he came to the door of the house and rapped out an unaccustomed oath.

"They've been here already," he said angrily. "Look!"

The marble table was overturned and broken into two pieces. The chair, that beautiful marble "throne" as the girl had described it, was overthrown from its solid pedestal.

"Now that's too bad," said Socrates angrily.

"My men wouldn't do a thing like this," protested the salvage officer, stepping over the ruins of the table. "Look, sir, what do you make of that?"

The base of the throne which Socrates had thought solid was in fact a hollow cavity and at the bottom was a flat tin box.

He stooped and pulled it out. The lock had been wrenched away and it was empty except for one sheet of paper, which the marauder had evidently left in his hurry. Socrates took the paper to the light. It was a title page, written in John Mandle's bold fist that he knew so well, and it ran:

Statement by John Mandle, ex-detective inspector Metropolitan Police Force, in regard to what happened at Pool-in-the-Moor, on February 27th, 1902.

Socrates sprang back into the summer house and made a quick careful search, but there was no other vestige of paper. The midnight visitor who had prowled around with an electric torch had done his work remarkably well.

The statement still existed, but in whose hands?

Workmen were hastily summoned and lifted the top of the chair back to the pedestal. It was uninjured, and the salvage man explained how unnecessary it had been to overthrow the top at all.

"It opens like a lid with the slightest pressure," he said, and illustrated his words. "Do you see? The back of the seat is mortised and the balance is so perfect that a push of the hand will throw the chair back and uncover the opening."

Bob was not at home when Socrates returned to Prince's Place. He owned a farm some ten miles away and had gone there to pay his labourers.

Lexington was discovered in a shady arbour and torn from the fascinating employment of holding Molly's wool.

"Sorry to interrupt you, Lex, but I have made rather an important discovery this morning," said Soc without preliminary, when he had got the boy into his room. "I have found the hiding-place of John Mandle's manuscript."

"Have you found the manuscript?" asked Lexington.

"One sheet of it," said Soc. "Read that and tell me what you make of it."

His brother took in the contents of the sheet at a glance.

"It's obviously the title page. Do you think the rest of the stuff was there?"

Soc nodded.

"Somebody had a particular reason for destroying this manuscript," he said, "and even went to the length of burning down 'The Woodlands' to effect that purpose. Evidently there was a trouble pressing very heavily upon John Mandle's conscience, and I should imagine that that, more than the fact that he had tricked Molly's mother into a bigamous marriage, was worrying him all the time and was responsible for his chronic state of nerves. What is more, he must have expected that the person against whose arrival he so carefully guarded himself would try to get hold of his confession, for a confession I am certain it was. That is why he kept his manuscript in the summer house. You remember that Molly told us be spent hours there, working, and was never interrupted save when he rang a bell to bring his servant."

"Then you think," said Lexington after a moment's thought, "that it was this person who was poking about in the ruins last night? It might have been Bob. He's interested in the case."

"Not sufficiently interested," said Socrates. "Besides Bob was with me all last night from dinner time until nearly midnight. It was half past nine when the unknown was seen."

"Jetheroe?" suggested Lex, and Socrates made no answer. "Do you think it was Jetheroe?"

"It might have been," admitted Soc.

"If it was Jetheroe," said Lexington, "and if Jetheroe had an interest in destroying this statement, he must have been the man who killed Mr Mandle."

"I shouldn't be surprised," was the evasive answer. "Lex, I wanted to tell you that I am engaging a new valet."

"You're not firing Septimus?" asked the astonished Lexington, for the aged Septimus had been his brother's servant for years.

"I can't bring Septimus down here. He wouldn't like it," said Socrates solemnly. "He doesn't approve of new places or new people. And it is his boast that he hasn't been two miles from Regent's Park in his life. No, I'm bringing down Frank."

"And who the dickens is Frank?" asked Lex.

"Frank is a model of all that a servant should be. He is a bachelor of arts and a bachelor of science. He has been secretary to two assistant commissioners and he looks like being a commissioner himself one of these days," said Socrates with a little smile.

Lexington drew a long sigh.

"Oh, I see. In other words, he is a detective."

"In vulgar words he is a split," said Socrates, "and I want him very badly around the house."

"Bob won't like that."

"Bob won't know," said Socrates. "I admit it's playing it low down on poor old Bob to bring a detective into his household, but I have instructions which must be carried out," he said humorously, remembering the message on the cheque, "and I don't think Bob is capable of affording Molly the protection which is necessary for her good health and well-being. Nor you either," he said, stopping the other's protest. "You're too much in love with Molly, and that addles your brain and distorts your judgment. No, Frank will do admirably."

"Of course, if you don't think I can protect Molly – " began Lexington.

"I don't," said the other briefly; "and more especially is this the case since you will not be here. Without making any further mystery about the matter," Socrates went on, "I am going into Devonshire to look at

Pool-in-the-Moor. I am especially interested in the possibilities which that dilapidated farm house may hold. And you're going with me."

"Oh, I see," said the young man relieved; "that is why you sent for Frank."

"That is precisely the reason," said Socrates; "and I may add that as Frank, to my knowledge, is engaged to a very pretty girl, the daughter of Staines, the pathologist, you need have no qualms about losing your lady."

Frank arrived that afternoon, a quiet, good-looking young man, and an ideal servant. He brushed and pressed clothes to perfection and was an instant success in the servants' hall.

"You don't mind my foisting another servant on you, do you, Bob?"

"Not a bit," said Bob Stone with a laugh when Socrates had explained the presence of his servitor. "But what has happened to that dithering old gentleman who used to look after you in Regent's Park?"

"Septimus is no traveller," lied Socrates glibly, "and he's not much of a worker in these days. I had to get this new man in on the pretence that he was looking after Lex."

Bob Stone nodded.

"Now come along to the study," he said.

Socrates had suggested the adjournment during lunch and the two men went along to Bob's cosy den.

"What is the important discovery?" asked Bob, and Socrates told him about the happening of the morning.

"So he kept his little secret under the marble chair, eh?" said Bob slowly. "What a queer fellow he was! What a queer fellow! Have you any idea as to what this manuscript contained?"

"Something particularly grisly, I expect," said Socrates. "I shall have to trace Mandle's movements on February 27th, 1902."

"I can save you a lot of trouble there," said Bob rising and going to a locked cupboard. "In 1902 Mandle and I were working more or less together, and I have a record of our movements. Not exactly a diary," he smiled. "Poor Molly, I suppose she hasn't found that diary of hers?"

Socrates shook his head.

"I used to keep just a brief record of my movements and the cases I was on," said Bob, unlocking the cupboard door and running his hand along a row of uniform volumes. "Here we are, 1902." He pulled down what was obviously a small office diary and turned the leaves. "'February 27th.' That was on a Friday," he said. "I was at Cardiff looking for the man Deveroux. I remember I searched an outgoing steamer bound for Bilbao."

"Was Mandle with you?" asked Socrates in surprise.

Bob nodded.

"Here is the entry," he pointed. "'Mandle and I searched SS *Antrim*. No sign of Deveroux.' We went back to London the next day. No, on the Sunday," he pointed out the entry.

"Then if anything happened at Pool-in-the-Moor on that day Mandle could not have been present. He must have learnt of it afterwards," said Socrates.

"Obviously," replied Bob. "Where is Pool-in-the-Moor? It sounds like Devonshire to me."

Socrates nodded again.

"It is a farm on the Ashburton road, the property of a Frenchman," he said. "So far as I can gather it is a derelict property and un-occupied."

"Why don't you go down and have a look at it?" asked Bob.

"I thought of going tomorrow," replied the other, "and taking Lexington with me. Did Mandle ever talk to you about the place?"

Bob Stone shook his head.

"Do you know what I think about Mandle?" he asked seriously. "I think he was mad."

"Mad?"

Bob nodded.

"He had all sorts of queer hallucinations. I don't for one minute believe that his life was ever seriously threatened, and I am certain that all those spring-guns and mantraps with which he laced the lawn, were symptoms of his monomania."

"He had good cause to fear," said Socrates dryly.

"You mean he was murdered? Yes, but isn't there a chance that the person who killed him was not the person — the imaginary person I daresay — whom he expected? Mandle was almost as furtive a fellow as you, Soc. He was always weaving mysteries about weird untenanted houses, and the sight of a dilapidated building was quite sufficient to start him speculating upon all sorts of mysterious crimes which may have been committed there. And don't forget that Mandle spent a lot of his time motoring through Devonshire. It was his favourite holiday place, and, as likely as not, he came upon this Pool-in-the-Moor and, struck by its quaint title, weaved some fantastic romance about it."

"I wouldn't say that was impossible," said Socrates thoughtfully, "but I'll go along and look at the Pool-in-the-Moor."

"You'll probably be very disappointed," smiled Bob. "Poor old Mandle. He is giving us a great deal more trouble after his death than he gave us before."

"By the way," said Socrates as he was leaving the study, "do you mind if Frank sleeps in my dressing-room? I am leaving behind a lot of little things which may have an important bearing upon the case if we ever get any further with it."

"Why not put them in my safe?" asked Bob. "But perhaps you'd rather not. Certainly let your man sleep there. He's a pretty useful fellow, but he doesn't clean boots very well," he said, dropping his eyes to Socrates' feet.

A little later Soc interviewed his grave manservant.

"Weldon, you're a rotten boot-cleaner. Bob spotted my brogues."

"I'm awfully sorry, Mr Smith," said the apologetic Frank, "but the fact is boots are my weak point. I'll take a few lessons when I get back to town."

"You'll sleep here, Frank," said Socrates opening the door of his dressing-room. "They'll put a bed there for you. You are now in the next room to Miss Templeton, and whilst I am away you will get all the sleep you can in the daytime and be alert at night. I would even suggest your sitting in the dark with your door ajar."

Frank nodded.

"Do you expect any attempt to be made on this lady?" he asked.

"I think nothing is more certain," said Socrates.

POOL-IN-THE-MOOR

He left early the next morning with Lex, and the girl motored down to the station with them to see them off. It was a long and tiring cross-country journey, and it was night before they reached Exeter. There was nothing to be done before the morning, and they were both too tired to be interested in anything but the comfortable beds at the Crown Hotel. But before he retired for the night Socrates put through a long-distance call and had the satisfaction of a chat with Molly – to Lexington's intense annoyance, for the young man did not know of this telephone conversation until later.

On arriving at Exeter, Socrates had received from the agent at Torquay exact instructions as to the location of Pool-in-the-Moor, and, after an early breakfast, they motored across Dartmoor, dipped down its steep street into Ashburton and climbed the hill on the other side of the town to emerge upon a wild stretch of moorland.

"That must be the place," said Socrates, consulting the letter he had received from the agent. He pointed to a building which stood against the skyline with no other habitation within sight.

There are very few trees on Dartmoor, but it looked as though the farm was surrounded by a close-set plantation. Socrates remarked upon this to the chauffeur, a local man whom they had hired with the car at Exeter.

"No, sir, they're not trees. That's the wall."

"The wall?" said Socrates in surprise. "It's a pretty high wall."

The driver explained that the owner of the property had had the wall erected by an Ashburton builder.

"It cost about twice as much as the farm is worth," said the chauffeur with a smile. "They call the place Frenchy's Folly round here."

As they drew nearer to Pool-in-the-Moor, the high wall became more apparent. It was so high that when the car drew under its shade, the farm building itself was lost to view.

"Not a very big place for a farm," said Socrates.

"No, sir," grinned the man. "It's not a farm at all, it's no more than a cottage. It gets its name from a pool of water about a quarter of a mile away, the only water this side of the Dart. There's a spring there, and a little brook drains it down to the Dart. You get some good trout fishing there sometimes," he added inconsequently.

Leaving the car by the side of the road, the two men made the circuit of the building. The enclosing wall formed, as nearly as Socrates could judge, an exact square. He paced off eighty feet in each direction. The wall was fourteen feet high and surmounted by a *cheval-de-frise* of broken glass, and the only opening in any of the four walls was a square stout door of weather-stained oak.

By walking a hundred yards back from the wall they could just see the red shingled roof and two squat chimneys.

"Now we'll take a look inside," said Socrates.

He tried the big key with its metal label, and at first it refused to turn. Socrates had foreseen something of this difficulty, and produced a cyclist's oilcan, the contents of which he sprayed into the keyhole. His second attempt was successful. The key turned with a snap, and the door creaked open for a few inches. Here they had some difficulty; for a small bush had grown against it on the inside.

"This gate hasn't been opened for twenty years at least," said Socrates after he had squeezed himself through. "Ask the chauffeur for the hatchet I bought at Exeter."

Lex came back with the instrument, and after some time they cut away the tough root of the bush and threw it on one side.

They were in what had once been a garden and was now a tangle of weeds breast high. The house was, as the chauffeur said, no more than a cottage. Its lower windows were shuttered and there was about the place an atmosphere of decay and desolation which even the brightness of the morning could not dispel.

"There is no use in searching the garden: I think we had better confine ourselves to the house," said Socrates.

He oiled the lock of the door which stood beneath a dilapidated stone perch. The key turned readily, the door opened without difficulty though its squeaking hinges set Lexington's teeth on edge.

They found themselves in a large hall, the floor of which was made of flagstones. Dust lay thick upon the oaken table and chair which formed the sole furniture of the passage, with the exception of a hanging lamp festooned with spider webs. From the hall gave two doors, one to the left and one to the right. The door on the left was not locked, and Socrates swung it open. There was a scamper of tiny feet and a chorus of squeaks.

"Mice, I think," said Socrates. "Rats would not live on the moor."

He turned on his pocket-lamp, and made his way across the floor to the window and, unfastening the shutters, flung them open.

The room had been sparsely furnished. It was impossible to judge the quality. The carpet on the floor had been half eaten away by generations of mice in search of warm nests, the walls were garlanded with dusty webs, and the dust lay so thick upon the pictures and the walls that it was impossible to see what they depicted. He went carefully round the walls taking in every object with his keen eyes.

"There's nothing here," he said, "let's try the other."

The door of the other room was locked, but there had been a key in the door of the room which he had just searched, and this, with some difficulty, he extracted. As he anticipated it turned the lock of its fellow. This proved a slightly larger room, with two shuttered windows which he hastened to unfasten. There was, too, a peculiarly musty smell of decay, which had been absent from the other apartment. A table in the centre of the room, thick with dust and debris, was laid as if for a meal. A chair had been drawn up at one end of the table, and on the left of the plate was a small black cylindrical object. Socrates blew away the enveloping dust which rose in clouds.

"A cigar," he said. "Look, it has burnt the table!"

There were still traces of grey ash amidst the dust, and the burn was easily discernible.

Socrates picked up the cigar and examined it closely. It was thin and awkwardly rolled. Not a kind which is usually smoked by English people. The chair was not set squarely, it was half turned as though the sitter had risen leaving his cigar behind.

"I wonder if we can find a broom," mused Socrates.

He went out and presently returned with one.

"Open the windows, Lex. I'm going to get a little of this dust off the floor."

He had not been sweeping for a minute before he stopped and bent down. The floor was of unstained wood, and his eyes had rested on something which had set his nerves tingling, an irregular black stain, the like of which he had seen before on many occasions.

"Look there, Lex!" he said. "That's blood!"

"Blood? Are you sure?"

"I shall be surer in a minute or two," said Socrates.

He knelt and scraped the floor with a penknife, and collecting the dust upon the blade, he emptied it into his palm and, carrying it to the window, examined it through a magnifying glass.

"Of course it's impossible to tell offhand, but I'm perfectly certain this is blood, and when we get back to Exeter I have no doubt that I shall confirm my first impression. Even with a glass I can see the crystallizations."

He went back and made further scrapings and placed the result in an envelope.

"That's blood," he said with conviction. "Now – whose blood?"

He looked around the room for a few minutes, but his scrutiny was not rewarded.

"I think I will finish sweeping this floor," he said.

There was a small patch of ragged carpet before the fireplace, but with this exception the floor was bare.

"Yes, it's blood. Look here, there's a patch there and a patch there. There's a trail to the door. We shall probably find traces in the hall."

He went outside and his prophecy was fulfilled. There were stains that probably led to the garden. On the doorstep, however, the weather had destroyed all further traces.

The two men returned to the dining-room, as apparently it was, and Socrates resumed his search.

"What's that?" he said suddenly pointing up. There was a round hole in the ceiling above the table, an irregular aperture about an inch in diameter. Socrates mounted the table and looked long and earnestly at this. Then he took his knife from his pocket and began probing into the cavity.

"Wood – an oaken beam probably," he said. "Pass up that light, Lex, I am going to enlarge the hole."

He cut away the plaster until the opening was wide enough for him to pass his hand through, and then flashed up the light.

"I thought so."

He dug gingerly with the point of his knife and something dropped in his waiting palm. It was a clot of dull metal.

"What is it?" asked Lexington.

"A bullet, and a bullet that has been through a body because it must have been already out of shape before it struck the beam."

Lexington stared at him.

"Do you think there has been a murder here?" he asked in a hushed voice.

"I think it is likely. Either a murder or – er – "

"Or?"

"Or an attempted murder," evaded Socrates.

He put the bullet into a matchbox, and then went upstairs. There were two rooms above, both containing beds, but only one was equipped with bedding, or what remained of bedding. A leather trunk stood open by the side of one of the beds, but it was empty. There was no sign of wearing apparel – not so much as a discarded collar. Moreover, what had evidently been a label inside the lid of the trunk had been cut away from the linen lining.

Under the bed was a suitcase which was also empty.

"H'm," said Socrates. "Travellers do not as a rule take away their clothing and leave their suitcases behind. I rather fancy we shall find the solution in the kitchen."

The kitchen was at the back of the house, a big low-roofed room, with heavily-shuttered and barred windows. It took them the greater part of half an hour to admit daylight into here. The first thing Socrates looked for was the fireplace. It was a great old-fashioned thing with huge iron firebars, and the interior was choked with ashes. Ashes overflowed, and mingled with the dust upon the capacious hearth.

By its side was a cupboard with coal and kindling wood. Socrates picked up a tin bottle and smelt.

"Paraffin," he said. "Somebody had a bonfire, and if that isn't the remains of a collar, my name is Jones!"

He lifted out a shred of ash and the shape was unmistakable.

"I wonder if there's been any burning elsewhere," said Socrates thoughtfully, and went back to the dining-room.

The grate was a large one and also was half-filled with ashes.

"He probably didn't make as good a job of it here," said Socrates hopefully, and removed the ashes flake by flake. He was rewarded, for wedged between two firebricks was a triangular scrap of paper, the base line of which was not more than half an inch in length. It must have been caught between the bricks and preserved from the flame by a simple chemical process.

Socrates took it out with a pair of tweezers and laid it carefully upon the face of an envelope.

Again he applied his magnifying glass, and Lex, looking curiously over his shoulder, wondered what there was in that tiny and apparently insignificant scrap to make his brother utter a startled exclamation.

"Look at that, Lex!"

Lex looked through the glass and saw nothing but a tangle of violet lines on a yellow background. They were the tiniest traceries and it looked to him like a portion of a label.

"Do you know what it is?" asked Socrates.

"A label of some kind."

"It is all that remains of a banknote, whether it was for a hundred francs or a thousand francs I cannot tell until I have put it before an expert. If you hold it up to the light you'll see just a suggestion of watermark."

"A banknote? Who would burn money?" said Lexington incredulously.

"Those who have money to burn," was the unsatisfactory reply. "There is nothing more to be found with the appliance we have," said Socrates. "We'll go back to the hotel and have a bath, and I rather fancy we shall need one."

They joined the impatient and now curious chauffeur, and they must have presented an uncanny appearance, for after his first shock of surprise he roared with laughter.

"There's some dust in there, sir," he said.

"We brought a little of it away with us," said Socrates.

As they were driving back the chauffeur asked him if he thought of buying the property, for it was in the role of prospective purchasers that they had made their search.

"I think it is likely," said Socrates. "Do you know a good gardener? A reliable man who would undertake to cut the grass and the weeds in the garden?"

"I'll take the job on myself, sir," said the chauffeur. "My home is in Ashburton, and I'm going there for a month's holiday next week."

That plan would suit Socrates admirably. He did not wish to bring too many outsiders into the business, and the chauffeur seemed a respectable, trustworthy kind of man.

"I'll send you a key down which will admit you to the gate," he said. "In no circumstances are you to go into the house."

He had closed the windows and shuttered them before he had left.

"I don't want to go into the house, sir," said the man, "but from the little bit I've seen of the garden it will want a lot of attention."

"You needn't bother your head with the idea that we're going to grow flowers," said Socrates. "All I want is the grass cut level, and I want somebody whom I can rely upon to collect and keep for me anything he finds in the grass."

He fixed up his arrangements there and then.

"And it's not a bad idea either," he said as he emerged from the bathroom an hour later a little more recognizable than he was when he had gone in. "If I brought people down from town there would be some talk. As it is, they look upon me as a possible purchaser, and it is only natural that I should want the garden cleared."

"What do you expect to find?" said Lex.

"Nothing very much," replied the other thoughtfully. "Only – well, one never knows."

"Have you any theory about this place and what happened there?"

"I have one or two theories – in fact I have three," said Socrates quietly. "Obviously the man who was killed at Pool-in-the-Moor was Deveroux, the Lyons bank robber, and I rather think that Mandle killed him!"

MOLLY GOES AWAY

"Killed him?" said the dumbfounded Lexington after he had recovered his voice. "But the man got away to South America."

"That also is possible. My theory may fall to the ground when it is submitted to the acid test of fact," said Socrates. "Remember that it is only a theory."

"But Bob Stone said that they were together at Cardiff on that date."

Socrates nodded.

"They may have been there on that date if you mean the 27th February, which is inscribed on Mandle's notes, but it doesn't necessarily follow that Deveroux died upon that date. After all, Bob Stone can only account for his own actions in conjunction with Mandle up to the Sunday when they returned to London. After that, if you had been as swift a reader as I am, you would have seen that Bob went for a month's holiday to Switzerland. It was about this time that the chief was feeling very sore with the pair of them for having missed Deveroux, and probably Bob jumped at the opportunity of getting away from the official eye."

"But what occurred on the 27th February?" insisted Lex.

"That we shall discover," was the reply.

They began the homeward trek that afternoon, breaking their journey in London, where they spent the night. On the following morning they started early, the earlier because an impatient Lex had tried in vain to get telephone communication with Hindhead the previous night. The line was either out of order, or, as the operator at

124

Haslemere had told him, the receiver at Prince's Place was off the hook.

"Are you going to tell Bob all you have discovered?" asked Lexington on their way down.

"No," was the unexpected reply. "In cases like these you can be hampered with too much information."

"I don't quite see how that can be," demurred Lexington, and his brother laughed softly.

"I'll give you an example, my innocent child," he said. "Suppose I tell Bob and suggest that this man has been murdered by Mandle. Bob will immediately set to work to prove by diaries and by other documentary evidence that Mandle could not possibly have been at Pool-in-the-Moor on that or any other day. Now, if there is one thing which I am not anxious, and which no police officer is anxious, to meet, it is an alibi to a charge which is not as yet formulated! I shall tell Bob that I have discovered nothing save a very dusty and untidy house in the midst of a poisonously rank garden. The rest will have to be slowly broken to him when I have the case against Mandle proved up to the hilt. And when I have that," he said after a moment's thought, "I think I shall have in the hollow of my hand the man who shot John Mandle on the night of the 3rd of June."

Bob was sitting on the broad terrace steps of his house smoking his morning cigar when their car swung up the drive.

"Hello, you're back," he said cheerily. "Did you have any luck?"

"Not a great deal," replied Soc.

Bob's eyes were fixed on the car.

"You didn't bring Molly back with you?"

"Bring Molly back?" said Socrates quickly. "What do you mean?"

"She went up to town yesterday afternoon," said Bob, and if he had dropped a bomb he could not have created a greater sensation. "I thought you had arranged it with her," said Bob. "She came in to me and told me that she was catching the 3.15, but as she was rather late for it, I offered to drive her to Guildford."

"Did she take any baggage with her?" asked Socrates.

"An attaché case. Why? Is anything wrong?"

125

"Nothing," said Socrates in a troubled voice, "except that she promised me she would not go away from here until I came back."

"That's strange," said Bob. "She quite gave me the impression that you knew she was going."

"Did she tell you where? Give you any address?"

Bob shook his head.

"I never troubled to ask her," he said.

Socrates went up to his room with a foreboding of evil. He found Frank brushing his clothes and closed the door behind him.

"Frank," he said in a low voice, "what has happened to Miss Templeton?"

"That's exactly what I've been asking myself all the morning," said Frank. "I went to sleep yesterday afternoon. I sat up all night as you instructed me, and I knew nothing about her going until about half past five, when one of the maids brought me up a cup of tea. I have a dim recollection of hearing the car going down the drive and I have since questioned the servants. The only thing they know is the time the car went and the time it came back."

"Didn't Miss Templeton tell you she was going?"

Frank shook his head.

"As a matter of fact, I had a talk with her. I went to get a book from the library and found her reading there. She asked me if I'd heard from you and I said no. She also asked me if I would take a nail out of one of her evening shoes which was hurting her."

"And she made no mention of going to town?"

"None whatever. She left me with the idea that she was staying here until you came back. When I left her I heard the telephone bell ring in the library, but I did not see her again."

Lexington and his brother exchanged glances. The boy was deathly pale and seemed suddenly to have grown old. Socrates gripped his arm affectionately.

"Probably some summons to town. Maybe it is her lawyer who called her," he said; but a telephone enquiry of the solicitor and every other likely telephoner disclosed the fact that none of these had communicated with her on the previous afternoon.

126

"I am taking no risks," said Socrates. "Report her as missing to the local police, and get a message through to Scotland Yard, Lex."

"I feel I have failed terribly," said Frank disconsolately.

"How could you foresee this?" demanded Socrates. "You carried out my instructions. I never dreamt she would leave in the daytime."

"Do you think – " began Lexington.

"I think this is serious," Soc answered the unasked question. "The previous disappearance was nothing and was simple to understand. This present affair – well, I don't like it."

Bob was distracted.

"Did you take her on to the platform?" asked Soc, "or did you leave her at the entrance of the station?"

"In the booking-hall," said Bob. "What a fool I was not to ask her – "

"Why should you ask her anything?" snapped Socrates, whose nerves were beginning to get a little thin. "Guildford Station is a pretty busy place, and I don't suppose there's any use in questioning the staff. There must be five thousand people pass through the station in the course of the day."

"I'll drive over and make inquiries," said Bob. "And I'll work round the villages in case – "

"In case what?"

"In case she came back," said Bob frankly. "I don't know whether she was going to London or whether that was a subterfuge."

"What do you mean?"

Socrates swung round to face him.

"I mean that Jetheroe may be at the bottom of this," said Bob. "Remember he's alive, he has some influence with the girl, and that there are reasons which I can't understand which make him keep in the background."

"Jetheroe," repeated Socrates. "I had forgotten him."

Bob went off soon after and did not return till late in the afternoon. He came simultaneously with a telegraph boy, who rode his bicycle up the drive hanging on to the back of the car.

"For me," said Socrates, and tore open the buff envelope.

"From Molly!" he said in surprise, and read:

Please come at once to 479 Quaker Street. I am quite safe but have made a wonderful discovery. Bring Lex and tell Frank, Janet wishes to see him.

"Janet?" frowned Socrates. "Who the dickens is Janet?"

"She's safe at any rate," said the joyful Lexington and Bob was one broad smile.

Socrates found his "servant" and handed him the telegram and saw him blush.

"Who is Janet?" he asked accusingly.

"Janet is my fiancée. How the dickens did she get into touch with her?" he asked wonderingly, "and what does she want?"

"Does she live in Quaker Street?"

Frank shook his head.

"She lives very close to Quaker Street, in Portman Square," he said.

"Well, there's only just time to catch the train. Rush your clothes on, Frank, and we'll go up together. Maybe we're going to have a revelation of the second mystery – for there are two."

"Two!" said Frank with a groan, "there are twenty-two."

The train was pulling into Waterloo Station when Socrates, without any warning, struck his knee with his fist.

"Hell!" he said.

It was an unusual expletive from Socrates, who seldom used very strong expressions. Frank, who was sitting opposite to him, looked up from his magazine.

"What is wrong, Mr Smith?"

"Nothing, except that I'm a fool," said Socrates bitterly, and then asked: "Is your engagement widely known?"

"What a question," smiled Frank. "I suppose it's widely known in our own circle. Our engagement was announced last month."

Socrates groaned.

"And I'll bet your portrait appeared together with the name of your fiancée and a beautiful caption under your angelic picture describing you as a promising official of the Criminal Investigation Department!"

"There was something like that," said Frank after a moment's thought. "Why?"

"I'll tell you why." There was no merriment which showed on Soc's face.

They had some difficulty in getting a taxi, but eventually they were deposited before the gloomy portals of 479 Quaker Street.

"It looks to me as if we've made a mistake," said Lexington, pointing to the brass plate on the door. "This is a preparatory school for children."

The maid who answered the summons seemed very surprised to see the visitors. It was in fact a preparatory school and the head master was in his study. He came down and Socrates briefly explained the object of his visit.

"There is nobody here except myself and my wife," said the master. "Are you sure you have the right address?"

Socrates took out the telegram and showed it.

"Yes, obviously that is 479, but the person who sent it made a mistake."

"One moment," said Frank suddenly, "let us go to my fiancée's house. It is just round the corner."

And there they learnt the worst. The pretty girl whom they interviewed had not seen Molly and did not know of her existence. She had certainly been no party to sending the telegram. It was a fake.

"Of course it was a fake; I knew it in the train," said Socrates bitterly.

"But why?"

"They wanted to get us away from Hindhead for some reason, Lex. We've got to get back there just as quickly as we can."

They had started for town late in the afternoon and they had missed the last of the fast trains of the day. It was only by stopping off at Guildford and hiring a car that they reached Prince's Place at half past ten. Bob was not there, but his servant handed two notes to Socrates, the first of which he tore open and read. The letter was written in pencil and apparently in a hurry.

DEAR SOC,
I have just had a telephone call from Molly herself. Apparently she is not in London but is at Weston-super-Mare. I am going straight away to find her.

Socrates folded the note slowly, and did not raise his eyes from the floor for several minutes. Then he opened the second note. It was from the Haslemere post office. He looked at Frank and smiled.

"The message from Weston was, too, I'll bet," said the young man. "It's lucky we got back. I wonder what their game is?"

"I wonder?" said Socrates softly.

He looked round at the butler, and they saw a hard little smile in his eyes.

"I'll bet you anything you like, Williams," he said flippantly, "that there is a concert or a cinematograph show in Haslemere tonight?"

"That's right, sir," said the man in surprise.

"I will also bet you that you have been bottling wine."

"Quite right, sir," said the surprised man.

"It isn't quite fair to spring that on you because I heard Mr Stone talking about your decanting the wine this morning."

And then be turned abruptly from the man, and walked up the stairs, and they stared after him.

"Now what the devil has old Soc got on his mind?" asked Lexington.

Later when he went upstairs he found his brother lying on the bed, fully dressed, but fast asleep. Socrates knew that there was a sleepless time coming for him, and although he was prepared to flirt with Fate, he was not ready, at his age, to take liberties with Nature.

Besides which, though this the younger man did not know, he had learnt the name of the person who had put through the telephone call

130

on the afternoon Molly had disappeared. The note from the post office had run:

Call to Prince's Place at 3.40 was from Jevington Institute, London, Marylebone 7979.

Therefore Socrates Smith slept soundly.

Lexington and Frank sat up all night, and they were looking haggard and tired when Soc came down the next morning fresh as paint and almost cheerful.

"Is Bob back?" he asked.

Lexington shook his weary head.

"Well, go along and sleep. You didn't expect him to get back from Weston-super-Mare in the night, did you?" he demanded sarcastically. "Bob will return at 9.30," he added, and he was extraordinarily accurate.

At a quarter to ten Bob's big limousine, white with dust, swung up the drive, and Bob, red-eyed and husky with sleepiness, heaved himself from the driver's seat.

"I took the limousine because I thought I should bring her back," he explained drowsily. "My God! I've had a night."

"Have you found her?" asked Lex eagerly.

Bob shook his head.

"I was fooled," he said. "That's all I can say, just fooled. Have you any idea what it's like, the road between here and Weston? Try it on a dark night, and keep your machine going at thirty miles an hour if you can."

He turned as he entered the hall.

"Any news?" he said.

"None," said Socrates.

"I'm going to have a bath and a sleep," said Bob, and disappeared.

"And I think you boys had better do the same," said Socrates. "I'm going for a turn round the garden."

"I'll come with you," said Lex.

"Personally I am not a bit sleepy," Frank volunteered this information, "and a ten-mile walk wouldn't do me any harm at all."

"I think the circumference of the garden will be sufficient for you," Socrates smiled.

They followed the path which ran parallel with the front of the house, and were turning to make the broad shady avenue of ancient hawthorn, when Frank stopped and his eyes grew round.

"What's the matter?" asked Socrates, and looked in the direction at which the youth was staring.

In the very centre of the smaller path which turned with the house was a shoe, a woman's shoe.

Socrates pounced upon it and picked it up.

"Molly's!" he said harshly. "Molly's, by God! And it wasn't there yesterday morning because I walked this very path!"

Frank was on the point of speaking, but Soc, with a gesture, silenced him.

"I want to be alone," he said, impatiently. "Now will you do me a favour? Go to your rooms and sleep. I don't want to see either of your faces till one o'clock this afternoon, and by gosh, if you knew what's coming to you, you'd be sorry to leave your beds."

THE STRANGLER

Three men slept heavily whilst Socrates Smith pieced together theory to theory, destroying that rough edge, fitting this into the pattern. The night before he had solved the mystery of Molly's disappearance, but he had thought she had gone willingly. The shoe told another story. She had kicked it off and left it there, a pitiful signal of distress, and the sight of it had roused the devil in Socrates Smith, that latent devil that had only shown on the surface twice in his life. Yet though she be in the deadliest danger, though she die, he could not rush events.

"The thing must bake," was his formula, but he watched the baking in a panic of fear.

Certain facts had yet to be made clear, and impatient of delay, he telephoned a taxicab and was driven to Haslemere. He was at Scotland Yard closeted with the chief of the Record Department, and on his way back before Lexington wakened from his heavy sleep.

Now, thought Socrates, now! He had in his hands the final threads of the mystery.

His train, a "non-stop" to Guildford, slowed outside Clapham Junction, and an electric local came abreast and moved at the same pace as the express. Glancing idly into the opposite carriage the eyes of Socrates fell upon a face and be leapt up.

It was Jetheroe! The man turned his head. His temple was still covered with plaster strips, and for a moment his eyes met Soc's, and then he turned his head away.

Socrates let down the window, but by this time the trains were speeding away from one another, the one to a distant platform at Clapham Junction the other to rumble through the station.

Jetheroe! For a moment Socrates thought of pulling the alarm cord, but he realized the futility of such an action. Before the train could be stopped or he could explain his business the electric would have started, or Jetheroe would have disappeared into the crowd of passengers which those local services disgorge at Clapham.

"No, I haven't disappeared, too," he said a little sourly when Lexington met him at the end of the drive. "I've seen Jetheroe! Is Frank awake?"

"He's up," said Lex. "Any news of Molly?"

Socrates shook his head.

"I want to see Frank. Tell him to come to me in the garden. Where is Bob?"

"He's not up yet."

Socrates nodded again. He was joined a little later by the spruce Frank.

"Do you want to see me, Mr Smith?"

"Yes, Frank. Do you remember the Jevington Institute prosecutions about seven months ago?"

Frank nodded.

"I was concerned in the prosecution," he said. "The Jevington Institute was an unlicensed private lunatic asylum run by a woman named Barn. And some queer things were happening there."

"What did she get?

"Six months hard labour," said Frank.

"That's five months ago. She'd be out now, wouldn't she? They remit a certain amount of the sentence for good conduct.

"I phoned there this morning and the man in charge of this precious institute informed me that Mrs Barn was away on a case. Of course, that may be camouflage for her still being in prison. Go up to London straight away, get on to this man who is probably her husband, find out where is Mrs Barn, and don't leave her until I give you further orders."

"Do you think she's in this business?" asked Frank in surprise.

"It's the wildest guess on my part," confessed Socrates. "But I've gone carefully into the matter and searched my soul this morning, putting myself in the place of the murderer, and I have decided that if there was one person in the world I should employ in certain circumstances that person was Mrs Barn. Now get away at once. Telephone me tonight. You'd better telephone the Haslemere Police Station, and I'll call for the message."

Frank nodded and turned on his heel. They did not see Bob until late in the evening, and he still showed signs of his strenuous night. The hand that poured out a stiff whisky and soda shook a little.

"Bob, you're getting old," bantered Socrates, and the other turned round on him almost offensively.

"I'm not so very old, Soc," he growled, "and anyway I don't want to be reminded of my increasing years."

Later Socrates informed Lex that he thought he had offended their host.

"Old Bob's sulking in his study and has sent out word that he's not coming to dinner," he said. "So you and I will dine in state. Lex, you mustn't let this thing worry you or you'll go mad," he said, seeing the misery in the boy's face. "Just keep your pecker up and have a little patience."

"A little patience!" groaned his brother. "Patience when Molly is – Heaven knows where!"

"After dinner you shall play me piquet," said Socrates with that queer smile of his. "There is nothing like piquet for easing, calming and soothing the nerves."

Poor Lexington was in no mood for cards, but his brother bullied him into the drawing-room, and the obliging Williams produced a card table.

"I suppose Mr Stone is not coming out of his study tonight?"

"No, sir," said Williams. "Mr Stone is very tired and is not feeling well. I have just taken him in his coffee, and he asked me to apologize."

135

Soc nodded. They were in the midst of the second game when Socrates put down his cards and raised his head in a listening attitude.

"What is it?" asked Lex, but the other silenced him with a look. He walked to the drawing-room door and opened it.

There was a side passage leading from the main hall, and at the end of this was Bob's study, which adjoined the library.

"I hear nothing," said Lex.

The words were hardly out of his mouth when there came from Bob Stone's room a yell that ended in a strangled "Whoop!"

In a second Socrates was racing down the passage with Lex at his heels. He flung himself against the door of the study. It was locked.

"Open the door!" he shouted and standing back took a running leap, flinging the whole of his weight against the door. With a crash it burst in. Bob Stone was sitting at his writing-table, his face was blue-black, his eyes were starting out, and his tongue protruded hideously.

He was clawing feebly at his throat around which a white silk handkerchief had been twisted tightly, and Socrates entered the room in time to see, as in a flash, the figure of a man disappearing over the window sill. His first move was toward Bob. An ebony ruler had been thrust into the handkerchief, and it was the turning of this which had almost ended the man's life.

Socrates twisted the stick the reverse way and Bob fell with a gasp across the table, half dead.

"Look after him!" yelled Socrates.

Stopping only to switch out the light he crouched down by the window and peered out into the darkness. He caught a glimpse of a moving figure and fired twice. Then without hesitation he leapt out of the window, though he had no idea of the distance he was to fall. He scrambled to his feet and tripped through a bed of flowers and reached the lawn, only to find that the intruder had vanished.

A chauffeur and a gardener had run out from the garage buildings at the sound of the shot, and quickly Socrates explained the reason.

"Search the grounds," he said. "Bring the man to me if you find him."

He made his way back to the study. Bob had recovered, and as Socrates came into the room, moved his arm a little nervously to cover a paper which had lain upon the blotting paper before him as he sat. The ink was still wet on the letters, Socrates noticed, for Bob's move to conceal the paper had been just a fraction of a second too late. There were only four letters, "Pool," but they explained a great deal.

Then it was that Socrates found that Bob's left hand was tied to the leg of the chair, and only his right was free. A strap had been passed round his waist, and he must have been helpless in the hands of his unknown assailant.

It was a long time before he could give a coherent account of what had occurred.

"I was sitting here writing," he said. "In fact, as you see, Soc, I was thinking about that infernal Pool-in-the-Moor house, and was idly printing the name, when I heard a voice from the open window say 'Hands up!' I looked round. There was a man whose face was covered, but whom I instantly recognized as Jetheroe. With surprising ease he climbed through the window, and holding me at the point of a gun, just long enough to lock the door, he forced me into the chair and fastened me as you saw. I knew it would be death to cry out, and I was hoping that somebody would come along, either Williams or yourself, and then before I realized what was happening he had slipped this scarf round my throat. I was helpless, but I struggled a little."

"That was the first sound I heard," said Socrates. "What happened then?"

"He tightened the handkerchief and I yelled."

"And that is all?" asked Socrates softly.

"All?" replied Bob. "What else? I've told you everything."

"Why didn't he strangle you without all these preliminaries?"

"Ask him?" snarled the usually genial Bob Stone. "Forgive me, old man, but my nerves have gone. What with Mandle's death and Molly's disappearance – " and without warning he dropped his head on his arms and his shoulders shook.

"I'll leave you a minute, Bob. I'll come back a little later," said Socrates.

He went back to the garden to find that the two men had conducted their search unsuccessfully.

"All right," said Socrates. "I'll have a look round myself."

There was no sign of the intruder, and he returned to the house. Lexington met him in the hall.

"Lex, go into Haslemere to the police station – I asked Frank to telephone there tonight if he had any information for me."

He found Bob so far recovered that he was taking an interest in the smashed lock.

"Soc," he said, "you're twice as strong as anybody would imagine."

"But not twice as nimble," smiled Socrates, "or I should have caught Mr Jetheroe, and I should have taught him that it is very bad form to attempt to strangle eminent ex-inspectors of police."

Bob chuckled.

"That was a narrow squeak, Soc. I would have given a great deal of money to have had one fair shot at our old friend."

He paced the room moodily.

"I can't help thinking that they'll have me yet," he said.

"Who are they?" asked Soc.

"Jetheroe and his crowd. The people who are behind him and working with him. The people who killed John Mandle and who have spirited away Molly. This is very nearly the strangest case you and I have been on," he said.

"Very nearly," agreed Socrates; "and if I could be sure in my mind that it was only one case and not two, only one plot and not a plot within a plot, I should be a much relieved man."

"What do you mean?"

"I'll tell you some day," promised Socrates, with a twinkle in his eyes. "The point is now, that I lack the necessary switches which connect the Three Oak Mystery with Molly's abduction."

"You're not sure that she's abducted yet."

"I'm fairly certain about that," said Socrates Smith calmly. "Molly was taken away from this house yesterday."

"Good God! You don't mean that!" said Bob huskily. "She left the day before!"

"She was in this house until yesterday, I repeat," said Socrates. "And all the time we were fooling around, running here and there in search of her, she was a prisoner in this very house. The wire that took me to London and took away my servant, Frank, who, as you know, is from Scotland Yard, was faked in order to get me out of the house."

"And the telephone message I received from Weston-super-Mare had the same object!" said Bob. "But where could she have been?"

"Let's make a thorough search of the house. Probably she has left behind her some trace. We'll start here," said Socrates.

"Here?"

Soc nodded.

"Where does that door lead to?"

"That leads to the library," said Bob, "and the other door to my swimming-pool. Not much of a swimming-pool," he said apologetically. "There is just enough water to let me swim a couple of strokes. You haven't seen it, have you?"

He opened the door, switched on the lights, and showed them into a big airy room, the walls of which were of white glazed brick. In the centre was a sunk bath about ten feet long by eight broad.

"What is in that cupboard?"

Socrates pointed to two white doors at a farther end of the room.

"My bathrobe. Nothing more."

Bob led the way and opened the door for inspection.

"What is this chair in here for?"

Bob scratched his head.

"I'm blessed if I know. I've never seen a chair in there before," he said.

Socrates looked round the room. The windows were high and beyond the reach of even a tall man.

"When were you here last?"

"I haven't had a swim for over a week," said Bob.

"And you haven't been in this room?"

Bob shook his head.

139

"And that door – where does it lead to?"

"That leads to the garden. As a matter of fact I built this at the same time as John Mandle built his study, and I followed almost the same plan, except that there is one entrance from the garden and one from my study. In his case he had an entrance from the bedroom down a flight of stairs. It was whilst his annexe was being built that the idea occurred to me to run up a swimming-pool for myself."

"Who else has access to your study?"

"Most of the servants," replied Bob. "Williams is here very frequently."

"And to the swimming-pool? Do you allow your servants to use it?"

Bob shook his head.

"Rather not," he said with a smile. "No, nobody uses this except myself. In fact there's no need even for the servants to clean it. The bath is automatically fed and emptied."

They came back to the study, and Socrates Smith stood before the fireplace looking at the tiny fire there, his hands behind him, deep in thought.

"Well, at what conclusion have you arrived?"

Socrates looked round to see if his brother was there, but remembered that Lex had gone down to the station to meet Frank.

"Bob," he said slowly, "there are two mysteries. One, at least, I have cleared up. I know why Jetheroe came to you tonight. I know exactly what he asked you to do. I know about the woman Barn of the Jevington Institute, and I know pretty well what has happened to Molly."

Bob did not answer.

"Now I'm going to tell you, Bob Stone, just a little story which I guess will interest you almost as much as it interests me. I am cutting out the Mandle murder and excluding that from my calculations. This is a tale of a man of fifty-five who loves a girl of twenty-two, and sooner than see her carried off by a younger man has committed the most infamous crime."

Bob's face was deathly white.

"I'll start with what I discovered two or three days ago, in fact the day after Mandle was murdered. For the moment I acquit you of that murder, because, from your point of view, it was perfectly senseless and there was no motive."

"You acquit me of the murder, do you?" said Bob Stone with a little smile. "Well, that's something! Maybe you'll acquit me of something else before you're through?"

"On the day following Mandle's murder," said Socrates as though the interruption had not occurred, "I came to your house to see you and you were in your library telephoning. You were telephoning to somebody named Barn, and I heard you say: 'It will be worth £500 to you.' Later you used the word 'Jevington,' all of which I heard, for I am a perfectly shameless eavesdropper. There is a man at Scotland Yard who never forgets anything. You probably know our old friend with the white beard and the spectacles who sits all the time in the Record Office storing information against the day of judgment. Well, I was so interested that I got into touch with him, and he told me the story of Jevington's and the story of the woman Barn, and I put two and two together."

"And made five!" sneered Bob.

"Just the same old four," replied Socrates easily. "You were in love with Molly, and Molly didn't love you. She had the bad taste to love a brother of mine, and personally I think it is an admirable choice. You were not quite certain about Molly and her feelings toward Lex, but you had already made up your mind that in certain eventualities you would take the bold step of carrying her off. Probably you had reached this decision before Mandle's death, but that is immaterial. I grant that it is a terrible experience to love, as you love, a woman younger than yourself, and to find your suit rejected. It is one which I have never had, but God gave me an imagination. As I say, you weren't certain just how Molly felt toward my brother, and that day we were at the inquest and I was discussing things with the assistant commissioner, it came out that Molly kept a diary, in which, girl-like, she put her tenderest thoughts.

"The proof of that was her anxiety to save the book when the house was on fire. Elderly people save their false teeth in similar circumstances," he added humorously, but Bob did not smile. "When you learnt of that diary you decided that you would see it, and to that end you broke into and entered the Chequers Inn, frightened the poor girl out of her life, and carried off her diary. I should imagine she had said some rather sweet things about Lex."

Bob's face was grey, his eyes were hard and hateful.

"Damn him!" he said and his voice trembled. "If he hadn't come down here – "

Socrates shook his head.

"My dear good fellow," he said gently. "If Lex hadn't come here there would have been another Lex, or a Tom, or a Jim, or a Harry. It was not ordained that Molly should be yours. With that book in your possession you fed the mad fury of your love for this girl and your hatred of Lex, and you decided that you would carry out your original scheme. You probably got again into touch with Mrs Barn, who had been convicted of conducting an unregistered lunatic asylum, a very serious offence. She was a hard, reliable kind of woman who would do anything for money, the kind of guardian that you could desire for Molly if you carried her away. Probably you have described Molly as a lunatic: I see by your start that you have. I feared this, Stone," the voice of Socrates had taken a new and a sterner note. "I brought an officer from Scotland Yard to protect the girl whilst I was away, and by your ingenuity you must have discovered that he sat up all night and spent most of the day in bed. The last seen of Molly was in the library next to your study. She was there reading and was not seen again by any member of your household."

"You're working up quite a case against me, Socrates Smith," said Bob Stone with a twisted smile.

"Am I not?" said Soc. "Yes, I am working up quite a case against you, and it's a pretty bad case too, Stone. As I say, the last seen of the girl was in this library. Frank saw her, and as he left heard a telephoned message. That message was from Mrs Barn. Nobody saw Molly again. It is true that your car was seen going down the drive, and that you may or may not have gone into Guildford. You certainly did not carry Molly with you. At that time she was in your swimming-pool, or, what is more likely, in the cupboard. I am not sure whether you drugged her or not. You probably did. At any rate, either by threat or persuasion you kept the girl quiet until you could get us all away from the house.

"When, like a fool, I'd fallen into the trap and disappeared – you motored to London and sent the wire – you carried her away under the pretext of having been summoned to Weston-super-Mare. The exact distance you travelled between eight o'clock at night and half past nine the following morning was 312 miles which, roughly, is the distance from Prince's Place to Pool-in-the-Moor and back."

Bob Stone licked his lips.

"It is also the distance from Prince's Place to Weston-super-Mare and back," he said, "by the way I went."

Socrates nodded.

"The girl is now at Pool-in-the-Moor, under the care of Mrs Barn. What your future plans are, I cannot speculate upon."

"What are you going to do?" asked Stone coolly.

"I am going to release the girl first," said Socrates, "and then I am going to take counsel with Scotland Yard as to what shall happen to you."

"H'm," said Bob Stone and smiled. "In those circumstances, you'd better know a little of the truth, in order that your wild fancies shall not quite destroy you, old friend and comrade. The thing you overlooked was this."

He led the way briskly into the bathroom and across to the big cupboard where the chair still stood.

"You want the truth. Now you shall have it. I brought her here as I bring you, and I said to her, 'If you move, if you utter a sound, I'll shoot you.' "

Bob Stone had been just a fraction of a second too quick, and Socrates raised his hands with that inscrutable smile of his.

143

"Now I know, Bob," he said, "that there is only one mystery." He glanced down at the automatic pistol in the man's hand. "You killed John Mandle."

The other's eyes were like steel.

"I killed John Mandle," he said coldly, "against my will. Just as I shall kill you. Get into that cupboard – quick!"

"I am a man of considerable intelligence," said Socrates, and obeyed.

The thick doors closed with a crash and two keys snapped.

"It will take me a quarter of an hour to pack my things," said Mr Robert Stone through the door, "and I shall be in the study all the time. If you use your gun to attract attention or to shoot away the lock I will come in and shoot through the panels and I guess I shan't miss you."

Socrates Smith said nothing. Not till he heard the whine of the big limousine pass under the high windows of the swimming-pool did he pull his gun.

WHAT HAPPENED TO MOLLY

Mr Robert Stone had a sense of the dramatic, and a sense of the dramatic occasionally leads a man from the straight and virtuous paths of truth. For the interview with Molly Templeton which he had described did not exactly follow his description.

Molly was in the study reading an interesting romance. Her mind, however, was less upon the printed page than upon the two men who were pursuing their inquiries in distant Devonshire, and really only one of these occupied the bulk of her thoughts.

She was sitting there when Bob Stone came in with his good-humoured face wreathed in smiles to answer the telephone. She paid no attention to the brief conversation, and presently he crossed to her.

"I have got a great scheme for you, Molly," he said. "What do you think I have been doing?"

"I can't guess," she said laughingly.

"I have been planning your wedding present."

She felt herself go red, but laughed.

"How exciting!" she said. "You're not going to tell me what it will be?"

"That's just what I'm going to tell you," he said. "You see I am designing the thing myself."

"What is it?" she asked curiously.

"A new kind of dressing-case. Only – " he hesitated. "I'm worried, because I don't know just what you will want in it."

"Show me the drawing."

145

"You'll laugh," he protested. "Now I'll tell you what, Molly. Do me a favour. Bring me down an attaché case with just the things you would ordinarily take on a short visit, say to spend the night with a girl friend."

"But why?" she asked in amazement.

"I want to take the measurements and get some idea – "

"I see what you mean," she said jumping up. "I'll bring you down a case with most of the things that I should take."

She returned presently with her attaché case, brushes and combs.

"And a suit of pyjamas if you will forgive the immodesty," she laughed.

"Bring them into my study."

He put the case on the table and looked at it thoughtfully.

"I ought to have asked you to bring your hat."

"But I shouldn't carry a hat in a dressing-case."

"That is the point about my dressing-case," he said solemnly; "and your umbrella."

She stared at him and burst into a peal of laughter. "I'll humour you," she said, and ran upstairs, to return with the articles he had named.

He was not in the study, but a door was open leading to a room into which she had not been. It was his swimming-pool, he explained, and she, who had not seen the place before, expressed her admiration. And then he suddenly shut the door and stood with his back to it, and the smile drifted from his face. She went on with what she was saying but she was shocked, and there was a cold feeling at her heart which she could not define nor understand. She finished breathlessly and waited for him to speak.

"Molly," he said at last, "you know I love you."

"Mr Stone, I thought that matter was finished with," she said quietly. "And it is hardly fair that you should tell me this under your roof."

"You know that I love you," he repeated.

"I know you think you do."

"I love you," he repeated. "I have everything I want in the world, Molly, except you, and I see no reason why I should not have you as well."

"I see many reasons," she said. "Will you please open the door and let me out?"

"I shall not open the door and let you out," he repeated her words almost mechanically as though he were saying a lesson. "You will not leave this room, Molly, until…"

She felt her knees give beneath her.

"I don't know what you mean," she breathed.

"I mean you are not going out of this room except at my wish and in my time."

"If Mr Smith – " she began.

"Socrates Smith will not know," he said simply. "When he returns I shall tell him that you went to town this afternoon."

"It's absurd," she burst forth. "How can you keep me here a prisoner? This is a silly joke of yours, Mr Stone."

"I'll tell you how I can keep you here as a prisoner," he said, picking his words with the greatest care. "Do you see that cupboard?" She turned her head. "It has a pretty thick door and I have placed one of my study chairs in there so that you shall not have too unpleasant a time. If you give me any trouble I shall put you in there and tie you hand and foot, and, if necessary, gag you, which will be unpleasant. If, on the contrary, you give me your word that you will not make a fuss, I will give you the free run of this bathroom. It is warm. I am afraid I must ask you to take your shoes off, otherwise people may hear you. This door is a double one," he pointed to the door leading to the study. "So I warn you it is quite impossible for anybody in the library to hear you if you bang on the panel, and if you did that, Molly – " he paused.

"Well?" she said defiantly.

"I should shoot you. Yes, though I love you I should shoot you with as little compunction as I shot John Mandle."

She shrank back from him, her hand in her mouth.

147

"You shot John Mandle?" she said hollowly. "You shot him? No, no."

He nodded.

"I shot him," he said. "I am not going to explain the why and wherefore of it. That is too long a story. But you may be sure I had good and sufficient reason."

He spoke as calmly as though he were explaining his choice of a particular make of motor-car.

"If I had to put the cause into a nutshell," he said thoughtfully, "I would say that I killed him because he was frightened of me."

"You're mad, you're mad!" she looked at him in horror. "You couldn't have done this, and if you did you would never tell me."

"I tell you, Molly, because I love you and you are going to marry me. I shall take you away from here, and when we have sent Smith back to town as mystified as ever, you and I will be together until – " he looked at her queerly, "until you decide that on the whole it is better that you should marry."

She passed her hand over her forehead. It was a dream she told herself, and yet she knew that it was all terribly real. Bob Stone, that charming, genial man, that "dear" whom she had never seen without a smile, whom everybody loved, whom his very servants adored! Bob Stone, the easy-going country gentleman, a murderer! The murderer of his lifelong friend! It was incredible.

"Now my dear," he said, "what is it to be? Are you going to be tied in the cupboard, or will you be sensible? Remember, if you make an outcry it is not necessary that you should die. It is certain that the person who happens to be with me in my study and who overhears you must not be allowed to carry the news. That person may be your dear Lexington," his lips curled.

"You're mad!" she said again, "mad! It was you who shot Mr Jetheroe?"

He nodded.

"Then you are – you are mad!" she gasped. "Mr Smith told me of that laugh that no sane person – "

Again he smiled.

"Mr Smith is a much shrewder person than you think, Molly. Socrates is a regular Socrates! He knew that that laugh was intended to shake his nerve and disturb his aim, but it failed. I was near to getting him, but by Jove, he was nearer to getting me! Look!"

With one hand he lifted the bushy hair at the side of his head, and she saw a white weal.

"That was Soc's bullet," he said with a grin. "It cured me of the habit of laughing too soon."

He looked at her.

"The cupboard?"

She shook her head.

"No, I'll be quiet. I think you'll come to your senses later and realize what a terrible thing you have done."

"Take off your shoes," he said, and she trembled angrily at his dictatorial tone. Nevertheless she kicked off her shoes, and he picked them up.

"You'll remain quiet here. I will see that your meals are brought in – by me, I may add," he said, as he saw a gleam in the girl's eyes.

"But you can't keep me here forever?"

"I shall not try to keep you here forever," he said. "I have a dear little home and a lovely little housekeeper for you," he chuckled.

A minute later he was gone, and she heard both doors locked with a sinking of heart. She took the chair and tried to reach the window. The windows were of heavy glass. Then she looked round for a missile of some kind. He had made most careful preparations for her captivity. There was not so much as a nail brush that she could use as a missile to attract attention from the outside. And she knew that he had spoken his mind and that it was no idle threat he had uttered.

Suppose Lex heard her. Her blood ran cold at the thought. She pulled the chair from the cupboard and sat down with her head in her hands to think out some solution, some means of escape.

There was no other door in the room. Yes there was! It was a door leading to the garden. She tried it, but knew beforehand that it was locked. If she hammered on the panels he would hear her just as if she were knocking at the door of the study.

Once she heard a motor-car and her heart leapt. Suppose Lexington and his brother had come back! But it couldn't be they, she realized, and dropped back to her listless attitude and her troubled thoughts. It was Bob Stone's car, and he was on his way to Godalming having carefully manoeuvred all his servants out of sight.

That night he brought her food on a tray and waited until she had finished eating, which was soon.

"You're not eating enough," he said. "I'll leave you some biscuits and milk. I'll bring you in a camp bed later."

He kept his word, and at ten o'clock he made her a bed, and bidding her a curt good night went out.

How that night passed she could never afterwards remember. She did not sleep, and welcomed the grey light of dawn that lit the windows. If the night had been long the day was interminable. She did not sleep. Once she thought she heard the voice of Socrates Smith, and her hopes rose, only to be dashed by the knowledge of her own impotence.

From sheer exhaustion she fell asleep later in the afternoon and wakened to find Stone standing over her.

"Get up," he said sharply and threw a heavy coat on the bed. "Here are some coffee and sandwiches. You'll want these."

"What are you going to do?"

"You're going a little journey with me."

"I'll not go!" she said, "I'll not go! I'll not go!"

"Don't be a fool," he said roughly.

"You can kill me," she cried wildly. "I'll scream for help if you lay your hands on me!"

Bob Stone smiled.

"You'd have to do some pretty tall screaming. I've sent all my servants into Haslemere to a cinema, and the only man in the house is Williams, who is busy in the cellar decanting wine. Now be sensible."

She had wakened hungry, and she ate the sandwiches and drank greedily at the coffee. She wanted all her reserves for the coming trial. Then an intense weariness overcame her, and she lay down again on the bed. She was awakened by a draught of fresh air in her face. Somebody was carrying her, and she was in the open.

The coffee had been drugged she thought dully. She could not scream. And then by a curious inversion of mind, she dwelt on one trivial circumstance. Had he put her shoes on? She felt for them. A shoe! In a flash the inspiration came! Socrates Smith had traced her once by her shoe.

Cautiously she raised the toe of one foot, put it against the heel of the other and pressed. The shoe fell and the next minute she was being lifted to a car. She sank back in the seat and almost immediately fell asleep again.

When she awoke the car had stopped. Stone was changing a wheel and cursing volubly. She had no clear recollection of any incident which followed. Only in the early hours of the morning she remembered coming to a gaunt house surrounded by a high wall and going, half walking and half carried, across a rank garden. She remembered, and experienced a momentary sense of relief, a woman who helped her to bed, and then she fell into a deep sleep which lasted for more than twelve hours.

IN THE HOUSE OF MYSTERY

Molly Templeton woke with a splitting headache. The room was dark, and there was no sign of windows. She afterwards found that blankets had been nailed up in lieu of blinds, for the upstairs rooms had no shutters.

She felt for matches and candle by the side of the bed, but her fingers found nothing, and the effort gave her such a sharp twinge of pain that she sank back again on the pillow with a moan. That sound must have been heard, for presently the stairs creaked under a heavy weight and the door opened to admit a woman who carried a kerosene lamp in her hand. She was a big bony creature with a square flat face and a hard mouth.

"Was that you talking, my dear?" she said. "Are you hungry?"

"I've an awful headache," said the girl.

"I'll cure that for you."

The woman disappeared, leaving the light behind, and was gone for some moments. She returned with a cup of tea and a little square box half filled with white tablets. The girl looked suspiciously at the medicine.

"Go on, it won't hurt you," said the woman harshly. "That's the worst of you lunatics, you always think people are trying to poison you." Molly stared up at her.

"Lunatics!" she said, hardly believing her ears. "Do you think I am a lunatic?"

"Of course you are. Don't you think I know one when I see one? Why I've been thirty-five years looking after nutty people."

In spite of her precarious position the girl felt a strong inclination to laugh.

"I'm a lunatic, am I?" she said, and choosing a cachet, put it on the tip of her tongue and washed it down with a sip of tea.

"Of course you're a lunatic. And if you only realized it you'd get better. That's what I always tell patients," said Mrs Barn complacently. "If you realize you're mad you can't be mad. That's scientific."

"How long am I to be kept here?" asked the girl. "Where am I?"

"In the fresh air and open country. A bit lonely, but none the worse for that," said the woman, and added admiringly: "My goodness, what a private home this will make!"

The girl looked at her wrist watch. It was five o'clock in the afternoon.

"Why, it must be quite light," she said in surprise.

"It's quite light," nodded the woman, and then Molly saw the blankets.

"Can't I see the light?" she pleaded. "I promise you I won't make any trouble or try to attract attention."

"If you cried till you was blue in the face," said Mrs Barn as she blew out the lamp and began unpinning the blankets, "you wouldn't be seen. If you expect to get a beautiful view you're going to be disappointed, my dear."

And so it proved. The evening sun lay athwart of the garden, and one big angle of blue shadow showed where the sunlight was cut off by the high encircling wall. There was no view save a tiny purple patch like an anthill that rose above the coping of one of the walls.

"Why, this is Dartmoor!" said the girl excitedly. "That is Hay Tor! And this," she looked at the wall and her mouth dropped, "this is Pool-in-the-Moor," she said in dismay.

"What a name for an institution!" said Mrs Barn ecstatically. "Now you get well as soon as you can, young lady, and clear out. I'm sure if I had a nice uncle like you've got I wouldn't want to stay here. It'll take a bit of putting into repair, mind you," she said half to herself, "and I don't know that you can do much with three or four rooms, unless you put two of them in together, and that doesn't do."

153

"Is this your place?" asked Molly in surprise.

"It will be."

And then the girl understood. Pool-in-the-Moor was to be the price which Bob Stone would pay to this terrible creature.

"When shall I leave here?"

Mrs Barn fixed her with basilisk glare.

"When your good husband comes and fetches you," she said.

"My husband!" cried the girl starting up, "whom are you talking about? You said my uncle just now, and I can understand Bob Stone pretending to be my uncle," she said viciously.

"It was your uncle who sent you, and your husband who brought you here," replied Mrs Barn with elaborate patience. "And a nicer gentleman you couldn't wish to meet."

"But I have no husband," she said wildly.

"That's your illusion," replied the calm flat-faced woman. "They all have them, especially at your age."

"This man has carried me away. Won't you please do something for me, Mrs – Mrs – "

"Barn is my name," said the woman. "I'll do anything you want, young lady, in reason."

"Won't you tell the police – Scotland Yard?"

A malignant look made the woman even more unattractive than she had at first appeared.

"I'll do a lot for Scotland Yard!" she said. She had a habit, when she was angry, of talking through her nose. "Oh, yes, I'd go out of my way to do a good turn to Scotland Yard, I don't think."

"But I've been carried away against my will. I've been abducted."

"That's your illusion, too," said the woman. "You're going to be a long time here," she said shaking her head. "Fancy turning on your good kind husband."

The girl's heart almost ceased beating. If this woman believed she was mad, if she believed Bob Stone was her husband, what hope was there for her when the man came?

She put her hand to her lips to prevent their trembling, for she knew that any kind of weakness shown to this woman, any evidence of fear, would further restrict her movement.

"Oh, he is coming down, is he?" she said with what coolness she could summon. "When do you expect him?"

"In two or three days," Mrs Barn nodded. "Now, what would you like to eat?"

The girl's inclination was to refuse all food, but that would have been really an act of insanity. She needed her strength, she had a desperate idea that she might be able to scale the wall, might even overcome this woman by some trick or other – to get the better of her by physical strength was a hopeless proposition.

"Bring me anything you have," she said. "Can I get up?"

The woman hesitated.

"Yes, you can get up," she said, "but you'd better dress while I'm here."

The girl rose. Her head was swimming but the throb had gone, and by the time she had finished her dressing she had regained her calmness.

"You've only got one shoe; I suppose you know that?" said Mrs Barn. "You'd better take a pair of my spring-sides."

She brought up a hideous pair of boots that squeaked with every step the girl took, an additional handicap in any plan she might form to escape from this prison.

To her surprise, when she suggested she should walk in the garden the woman offered no opposition.

Mrs Barn was trained in the art of "nursing" people of unsound mind, and knew to a fraction how much latitude could be allowed them. Moreover she had looked over the grounds with a professional eye, and had recognized the impossibility of an inmate escaping without assistance.

There were no ladders in the grounds, and the only way out was through the door which would be seen from the kitchen. The hall led straight through to that office.

Molly walked slowly through the high grass, stopping now and again to pick the wild flowers which bloomed in profusion, and all the time she was looking for some avenue by which she could gain her freedom. There was no tree in the ground though bushes were plentiful, and twice she walked round the house without discovering the slightest ground for hope that she could get away. The door through the wall was solid looking, and the lock was formidable. She looked up at the house. There was only one floor above the ground, though there was an indication of an attic in a gabled window at one end of the sloping roof. Could she get a message over the wall? When she got back to her room she searched for paper, frantically turned out her attaché case – how little she had dreamt of the use to which it was to be put when she packed it, she thought – but there was neither paper nor pen nor pencil.

She joined Mrs Barn at her frugal meal in the dining-room illuminated by the kerosene lamp which the woman had carried up to her. It was a cheerless room in spite of the little fire that burnt in the grate. It still bore evidence of neglect and decay, although Mrs Barn had spent hours in clearing out the dust and rubbish. This was her grievance, as the girl discovered.

"I'm not used to doing housework, and I wish you'd tell your husband when he comes – "

"He's not my husband," said the girl, but then, realizing the hopelessness of it all: "What am I to tell him?" she asked.

"That I'm not used to doing housework. It's menial. You have no idea what this house was like when I came into it a couple of days ago. I'd have gone home if it hadn't been I wanted to oblige you, dearie."

She might have added the consideration of a very handsome sum plus the use of the house which Bob Stone had given her in the one case and had promised her in the other.

"Now look at that ceiling." She pointed to the hole which Socrates Smith had cut. "That looks to me like rats, though I haven't seen any. This place has been neglected," she said shaking her head. "Look at those ink marks all over the floor. I haven't dared go down into the cellar."

"Is there a cellar?" asked the girl idly.

"There's two," said the woman. "Family vaults I call them, but they might do at a pinch for – " Her mind dwelt pleasantly upon some unfortunate patient of the future for whom the family vaults would provide at least a sleeping place.

The girl sat up till three o'clock in the morning. Her long sleep of the day seemed to have exhausted her capacity for slumber, and it was daylight before she fell asleep.

She went down to breakfast, a miserable meal of weak tea, bread and butter. The bread was cut thick, and the butter spread by a careful hand, and she was glad to get into the garden again.

She walked round and round the house till she felt dizzy, until every discoloured brick was familiar to her, until she had located even the ventilators of the cellars.

A talk with Mrs Barn that afternoon gave her an idea. The woman told her that these solitary houses on the moors had originally been owned by smugglers; and she spoke vaguely of great caverns underground that spread "for miles and miles," an obvious exaggeration, but it raised a pleasant vision to the girl.

"What can I do?" she asked at last.

"I'll tell you what you can do," said Mrs Barn unpleasantly, "you can take a broom and do a bit of sweeping."

Even this was attractive, but she could not continuously sweep the house, which was small.

"Can't I go and look at the cellars?"

"You can if you like. You'll find the key hanging on a nail."

The cellars proved to be most uninteresting. The light of a lamp revealed nothing more terrifying than an old mouse that darted through the ventilator at the first glint of light. There was obviously no escape from here. The second cellar seemed to be a replica of the first, until she saw something which raised her hopes to a higher pitch. The cellar was lined and floored with brick, and on one side the brickwork was apparently new. Moreover, it followed a roughly defined semicircle.

Suppose there were a passage there, she thought! But even if there were, how could she break down the brickwork? She looked round the cellar and her heart gave a little leap.

In the corner were a shovel and a pickaxe. Beneath two old sacks that sent out a cloud of white pungent powder when she moved them, was a trowel. She went upstairs again. Mrs Barn had removed herself to the garden, and seated in a deckchair, was taking the sun drowsily. She had chosen the place for her sleep immediately opposite the garden gate, so that it could not open without her being disturbed.

The girl went back to the cellar, and with trembling hands took up the pick. It was terribly heavy, and her first blows, aimed wildly, were nearly disastrous to herself. As she grew cooler she grew steadier. Presently she had prised out half a brick and had discovered that there was another course behind. She went upstairs and took a look at Mrs Barn. She was asleep. After half an hour's labour she had driven a hole through the brickwork and, wonderful to relate, there was a black cavity beyond!

There was no doubt at all about it. She held her lamp so that it showed through the hole she had made, and she could see neither earth nor stonework beyond.

If she could only get through under the wall she might dig her way up to the open she thought.

She heard Mrs Barn cough, dropped her tools, and brushing her hands, ran up in time to meet the woman halfway across the garden.

"Well, what have you been doing?" she asked the girl suspiciously.

It was her habit to wake up, even from the shortest sleep, in the worst possible temper.

"Just looking round," said Molly carelessly.

The woman grumbled something as she went through to the kitchen, and Molly, not daring to descend the narrow stone stairs which wound from the passage to the cellar level, went out and took Mrs Barn's place in the deckchair.

When should she make the attempt? That was the question. The time at her disposal was short, and though she resolutely strove to keep from her mind all the horrors which might follow Bob Stone's arrival, she could not altogether dismiss that picture.

Mrs Barn decided for her, all unconsciously. She was unusually gracious at the evening meal and mentioned one of her peculiarities.

"I always sleep with my door locked," she said. "I'm such a heavy sleeper, and I've had such vicious devils to deal with that I wouldn't dare sleep with it unlocked. Why, do you know, a young lady like you with similar illusions nearly killed me once!"

The girl shuddered, not at Mrs Barn's danger but at the picture of the poor soul "with similar delusions," and the terror which must have stood at her elbow all the time.

"You are a heavy sleeper?" she said carelessly.

"Pretty heavy. When I was at my other institution me and my husband took turn and turn about. While he was asleep I was awake. While he was awake I was asleep. You're not going to give me any trouble, are you?" she looked suspiciously.

"You'd better lock your bedroom door," said Molly solemnly, and the woman grunted and brightened up.

"Well, your husband will be coming for you soon, thank God!"

This decided the girl. She could work that night, and it helped her plan that Mrs Barn had unearthed another lamp from some kitchen cupboard.

Molly spent that night between hope and fear. It was by no means certain that the underground cavern, if cavern it was, would lead to safety. There was a chance that it might end in her being lost and perishing miserably underground. Her lips trembled. She was very young, and life was full of bright promise. Too young to die on the very threshold of happiness. She stilled these thoughts by an effort of will, and sat patiently waiting for Mrs Barn to retire.

At ten o'clock a heavy footfall passed her door, a voice growled "good night," and muttered a warning which she did not catch, but which she supposed had reference to any attempt to escape. She waited another two hours, then crept out and listened at the woman's door. She heard her regular snore, and went downstairs aflutter with excitement. She was dressed, but carried Mrs Barn's squeaky boots under her arm.

She had some trouble in finding matches to light the lamp, but presently she had it burning, and turning it low, she descended the steps and came to her cavern. She must proceed with the greatest caution. She aimed one blow, and the sound of it reverberated through the house. It was some time before she ventured to make another attempt. She found that by putting one end of the pick into the hole she had made and pulling steadily on the handle she could loosen the bricks. She had pulled out three in this way, when, taking a greater purchase and exercising a heavier pull, the whole of the wall came down with a crash. She stood up trembling with fear. Mrs Barn must be indeed a heavy sleeper if she failed to hear that roar of sound. The girl hesitated for a moment, and then, blowing out the light, she fled up the steps, and, as noiselessly as possible, mounted the creaking stairs.

She was closing her door softly when she heard the heavy tread of the woman crossing her room. A few minutes later Molly's door opened and the woman, a fantastic figure in a red dressing-gown, came in holding a lighted candle.

"What was that noise?" she grumbled.

Molly, the bedclothes drawn up to her neck, pretended to be asleep, and gave an artistic imitation of one aroused from slumber.

"What is it?" she asked.

"Did you hear a noise?" said the woman.

"No," replied the girl.

Evidently Mrs Barn was not satisfied; for the girl heard her going down the stairs. Fortunately Mrs Barn did not carry her investigations to the point of searching the cellars, and presently she came up again, and Molly heard her grumbling, heard too the click of her lock, and waited for another hour before she ventured from her room. Her sleep thus interrupted, Mrs Barn slept more soundly than ever. Her snores were now ponderous, and Molly, her fears having subsided, made her second visit to the cellar.

When she reached the hall below she listened. Even from there she could hear the woman's stertorous breathing. She had clung on to her box of matches, and she lit one to find her way down the steps to the cellar door. In a few minutes she had rekindled the lamp, and stooping before the opening, she began to loosen the bricks gently and to make the opening larger. Peering through, she could see no outlet, and she had a horrible suspicion that she had done no more than open a bricked-up recess.

There was something long and white and gleaming half hidden in debris and dust. She could not see what it was, and she delayed inspection until she had made the hole big enough to creep through. Then she lifted the lamp and looked.

The scream that rose to her throat she stifled by the greatest effort of will. The lamp wobbled in her hands and her eyes started.

She would not faint, she would not faint! she told herself desperately. Yet her very soul was screaming in terror, for the thing she had seen was now revealed. It was a human skeleton! Its hollow eyes were turned toward her, its gleaming teeth were set in a crooked grin!

THE MAN IN THE ATTIC

She backed away, still holding the lamp that shook and trembled in her hand, back, back to the door, and all the time it seemed that deep in those sockets were eyes that watched her.

She pulled the door to with a crash, and staggered up the stairs, and then she heard a sound above.

She needed all her courage to extinguish the lamp and remain in that fetid darkness, yet she mastered her fears, and blew shakily down the glass chimney. She was in darkness, illuminated by the oblong doorway into the hall.

Who was it? It was not Mrs Barn. Her snores were painfully distinct. No, it was somebody else. Somebody was in the hall. She heard stealthy footsteps. The mere shadow of a shadow passed the opening and was gone. Was her imagination playing tricks, or had Bob Stone come? This last thought roused her to a sense of her danger, made her for a moment forget the horror that lay behind her in the thick darkness. She waited awhile, then crept up to her room, closed the door behind her and sank shivering on her bed.

What awful secret did this house hold? What dark ghosts had their habitation in these dusty rooms which were so redolent of tragedy? The stains on the floor! She remembered them. Mrs Barn had called them ink-stains, but Molly knew now that they were blood. It came to her with tremendous force. Curiously enough this realization horrified her more than the concrete fact of those pitiful bones or the mystery shape that stole through the house.

The sun had risen before she fell into a troubled sleep, from which she was awakened by Mrs Barn.

"Here, come on, get up, young woman! I've brought you up a cup of tea, but don't you think that I'll do that every morning. It's your job to make me a cup of tea, and I'm going to tell your husband so."

She sat up, blinking and stupid.

"What is it?" she said dully and stared round.

It was almost a relief to see the flat yellow face of this awful woman. She at least was real, alive, tangible.

"I'm sorry, Mrs Barn," she stammered, taking the tea from the woman. "I'm afraid I didn't sleep very well."

"Your hand's shaking. What's the matter with you?" asked Mrs Barn suspiciously. "You're in a nice state if your husband comes down today."

Her husband! So it wasn't Bob Stone, that flitting figure. She had had a wild hope for a second, for the fraction of a second indeed, that it was Jetheroe, the mysterious Jetheroe, who shuttled to and fro in the web of her life; but this figure was shorter, a squat uncouth shape; she recalled it from her momentary glimpse.

"Could I have a bath?" she asked, and Mrs Barn was amused.

"You could if there was a bath," she said. "What do you want a bath for? You're clean enough. Wash your face and come down."

The water in the little ewer was cold and refreshing. The girl bathed her face until it glowed again, and though the drug of sleep was still in her and her limbs had an unaccustomed heaviness, she joined the woman at the breakfast table and was almost glad of the company. She did not wonder how Mrs Barn received her supplies. The food they had had evidently been brought from some town; eggs and cold pies, bottled preserves and condensed milk all spoke eloquently of preparation. The bread was just a day staler than it had been on the previous day. So tradesmen were not calling, thought the girl. In this surmise, however, she was wrong. At eleven o'clock came a rapping on the outer gate. Mrs Barn peremptorily ordered Molly into the house, closed the door upon her and went to answer the knock.

Through the window of the dining-room the girl saw the woman take in a basket of provisions, evidently from a tradesman. Of the tradesman himself she did not see any more than a hand holding a basket. Mrs Barn brought it into the dining-room with every evidence of satisfaction, and placed two large new loaves upon the table.

"Well, we're not going to be starved, anyway," she said, with the nearest approach to good humour she had shown. "What are you going to do this morning?" she asked suddenly. "Poke about in the cellars?"

"No, no," said the girl with a shiver, "no thank you. It's too – too cold down there. I'll just sit in the garden, I think."

The woman grunted.

"Can you cook?" she asked.

"No," confessed Molly.

"Well, it's about time you learnt," grumbled Mrs Barn.

She took the provisions into the kitchen, and later dragged out her chair and took up her position with her back to the gate, for her morning siesta.

The girl could not remain in the house alone. She wandered round and round the ugly building speculating upon its history. Who were its former owners? With what hopes was it built, what tragedies had it held?

Those bricks had been laid one upon the other in the days of the Napoleonic wars, when Dartmoor was alive with gangs of French prisoners of war. Possibly this house had been built by them.

Mrs Barn had left her chair and had gone into the house when the girl came round for the third time. As Molly passed the door she heard the woman shout:

"Here, missus, come here!"

Molly obeyed and went through the hall to the kitchen to find the woman standing, her hands on her hips, looking at the basket on the table.

"How many loaves of bread did I bring in?"

"Two," said the girl in surprise, "why?"

164

"Well, where's the other?"

She pointed to a loaf on the table. Its fellow had disappeared!

"Are you sure I brought two?"

"I'm almost sure," said the girl.

The woman looked round.

"There are no rats here and anyway they wouldn't take a loaf of bread."

The girl felt her heart beating quickly. That sinister figure she had seen in the dark! She wanted to laugh, but she wanted to cry as much. Her nerves were all jangled, and she was on the point of an hysterical breakdown, but happily recognized her own symptoms, and with an effort pulled herself together.

"Probably we were both mistaken, Mrs Barn," she said. "I'm so tired this morning that I am seeing things that aren't existing."

"I'm not so tired," said Mrs Barn. "You haven't taken the bread?"

"Why should I take it?" said the girl. "I'm not hungry and can have all I want."

"Well, that beats me," said the woman, and locked the provisions in a cupboard.

And now the girl made the round of the house no more. She felt nervous, frightened almost, and kept close to the woman, contenting herself with pacing the stretch of wild grassland in front of the door.

She was certain that there had been two loaves. She had noticed that one was burnt on the top and the other had been baked a paler brown. It was the burnt loaf which had disappeared.

"This house gives me the creeps," said Mrs Barn as they sat to the meal. "I'll be glad when my husband can come down – and your husband," she said, looking at the girl under her heavy brows.

Molly fetched a long sigh. She had almost forgotten Bob Stone in her own terrors, and had tried desperately hard to forget the only means of escape she had conceived. It was a house of horror, a house of whispers and creaks, of hidden ghouls, of lurking shapes – she dreaded the coming of the night.

She was pacing slowly up and down, Mrs Barn dozing in her chair, that afternoon, when she raised her eyes to the gabled window. She had seen it before, a triangle of dirty irregular glass covered with glazing which had been put in when the house was built.

What room was there, she wondered? She had seen a flight of steps running up to a trapdoor. The steps were almost opposite her own room, and Mrs Barn had told her that it was a lumber-room. And now as she raised her eyes she started and dropped the book she was carrying and screamed. At the window she had seen a white distorted face, just a glimpse, but it was enough. She sank to the ground in a heap.

Aroused by the scream Mrs Barn came waddling across the green. She lifted the girl to her feet, half-dragged, half-carried her to her chair, and flung her down savagely.

"What's the matter with you?" she asked. "Here, wake up!"

She shook her, but Molly showed no signs of recovering consciousness. Then, gripping the girl's neck with her big hands, she forced her head down to her knees.

Molly opened her eyes and looked wildly round.

"What's the matter with you?" were the first words she heard.

The girl staggered to her feet, and swaying, would have fallen again if Mrs Barn had not caught her.

"Are you going properly mad?" asked the woman.

"I am properly mad, am I not?" said the girl hysterically. She had recovered sufficiently to smile though her face was white as death.

"What made you faint?" asked the woman suspiciously.

"Nothing," said Molly. Perhaps it had been an illusion. The thick windows with their bosses of glass may have played a trick with her, she thought.

"I'll be glad when your young man comes," said Mrs Barn fervently. "What's the matter with you, hey?"

"I'm mad, am I not?" said Molly. "You told me so several times, and mad people can do almost what they like."

"They can do what I let 'em do," corrected Mrs Barn grimly.

That evening Molly summoned up her courage to ask a favour.

"Can I sleep in your room tonight, Mrs Barn?" she said.

"In my room?" said the woman astonished. "Not likely! Haven't I told you I don't allow mad people to get anywhere near me when I'm asleep?"

The girl laughed.

"You know very well I am no more mad than you are," she said.

"Whether you are or whether you're not you don't sleep in my room, where I keep all my keys," replied the other significantly. "You stay in your own."

"Have you a key for my room?" asked the girl.

"If I had you wouldn't get it," was the uncompromising reply. "No, you sleep in your own room, and get out of your squalling, fainting habits. Besides," said the woman with a little grin, "your husband may come tonight."

Molly's heart sank like a stone.

"My husband," she faltered. "What difference would that make?" and then she blanched afresh. "You're not going to let him come into my room?" she said breathlessly. "You know he's not my husband! You know!"

Mrs Barn rolled her head to express her weariness of the subject.

"That's your illusion. You poor little fool," she said, "that's your illusion."

Pathologists say that no brain can hold the impression of two pains, the greater must relieve the lesser, and in the new terror, real and vital, the mystery shape, that distorted white face in the garret, those mouldering bones in the cellar, were forgotten.

When she went to bed that night the girl did not undress, but lay, covering herself with an eiderdown which she recognized as having been on her own bed at Prince's Place. There was no means by which she could barricade the door. The only furniture in the room beside the bed was a flimsy dressing-chest and a washstand. She tried to pull the bed against the door, but it was one of those old mahogany beds, and she could not move it.

She would lie awake, she promised herself, but she had been awake all the previous night. She tried every expedient to prevent her weary eyes from closing, but at last Nature asserted herself, and she fell into a calm unruffled sleep…

"Wake up!" A big hand was caressing her face, and the voice was Bob Stone's.

She thought she was dreaming, and turned over on her side.

"Wake up, Molly!" There was no mistaking his voice this time.

She struggled into a sitting posture. Bob Stone, his face grey with dust, his long soiled coat covering him from shoulder to heel, stood by the side of her bed.

In the doorway she saw Mrs Barn in her red dressing-gown. It was dark. What time she could not guess. But the fact that Mrs Barn had been aroused from her sleep by the visitor suggested that the day had not yet broken.

"Get up," said Bob laconically. "You're dressed, eh? Well, that would make it very easy for me – "

"What do you want?" she asked in a terrified whisper.

"I want you, Molly, and I'm going to get you sooner or later."

He turned his head to the woman at the door.

"You can go," he said. "Shut the door."

"Don't go, don't go!" begged the girl.

She tried to run past him, but he caught her in his arms, and she heard the thud of the closing door. He was holding her tightly, his face, grimed with the dust of the road, looking down into hers.

"They found me out, Molly," he said. "Soc Smith is after me, and he'll be here in two or three hours."

"Here?" she said eagerly. "He knows I'm here?" she said, and he nodded.

"Oh, yes, Soc knows," he said softly, and he looked at her with a queer little smile. "I could take you now but I won't," he said half to himself. "I want leisure to court you, leisure to break down your silly resistance."

What was he going to do she wondered? His words were a reprieve.

"You'll learn to love me in time, Molly. We'll go away to a beautiful land – to Brazil. I have made all preparations."

"And if I don't love you," she said steadily, "and I refuse to love you? What happens to me? Do I share the fate of the man in the cellar?"

Before she had spoken the words she regretted them. Under the dust his face went old and haggard.

"The man in the cellar," he mumbled, "the man in the cellar? Good Heavens! You haven't found – that?"

She did not speak. What a fool she had been! What a fool to let him know! He gripped her shoulders savagely.

"Answer me," he roared. "What did you find? How did you find it? Does the woman know?"

She had to tell him of her wild scheme for escape, of her midnight visit to the cellar and what she had found there. As she progressed he grew calmer.

"You poor little thing," he said in a voice that was almost gentle. "I could have spared you that."

He meditated for a moment, biting his knuckles. "That old fool ought to have stopped your going into the cellar. I told her that she was not to take her eye off you."

He looked at his watch suddenly.

"I am going to Plymouth," he said.

"You're not – not taking me with you, are you?" she asked, and to her amazement he shook his head.

"I am coming back for you," he said.

"I think not."

Molly looked up as Bob swung round. A man was standing in the doorway, a man whose unshaven face was black with dust. A revolver was in his hand and she instantly recognized his voice, though she had not known him when she had seen him through the glass of the upper window, nor when he had flitted past her in the dark hall.

"My name is Sub-Inspector Frank Weldon from Scotland Yard. I shall take you into custody on a charge – "

A shot rang out. Bob Stone had fired from his hip and Frank pitched forward on his face.

The girl screamed. There was a clump of feet outside and the scared face of Mrs Barn appeared.

"Oh, what have you done!" she gasped.

Bob Stone did not reply. He slipped the smoking revolver into his overcoat pocket, and stooping, lifted the inanimate figure and bore it outside.

"Shut that door!" Molly heard his voice, and the door banged on her, leaving her staring at the red patch on the bedroom floor, where Frank Weldon had fallen.

She tore down the blankets that covered the window and flung open the casement. Stone was bearing his burden across the garden. She could see his white coat. She glimpsed the ugly figure of Mrs Barn and heard her whimper of fear; and then Bob disappeared through the outer gate, and the door was locked behind him.

"My God! My God!" Mrs Barn's whimper came up to her and presently Molly heard the sound of her feet upon the stairs.

The door was flung open and she came in, and the old woman's dismay would have been laughable had Molly the gift of laughter.

"This is murder!" she wailed. "This is police work! Why did I ever take his money! I never thought it was anything else but his wanting you! Curse you and your man, curse you!" she stormed. "Where did he come from, that split?"

"He was in the house all the time," said the girl with a trembling voice, and the woman wrung her hands.

"They'll know he's here. Scotland Yard will be down in the morning, and what am I going to do? What am I going to do? Look here, miss," she seized the girl's hands in hers and her drooping mouth trembled in its agitation. "You know I had nothing to do with this business, don't you? I had nothing to do with the murder. I only helped him to look after you. He gave me £500, and I was going to get this house. You'll speak up for me? I wasn't here when he shot that split, was I, my dear?"

"Go away, Mrs Barn," she said quietly. "I want to think."

The girl shook her head.

"But you'll speak up for me, won't you, miss? You know I had nothing to do with this shooting. He's taken the body away. I hope he doesn't come back again. I hope not. You'll speak up for me if it comes to a trial, won't you, my dear? Let me get you some tea."

This hideous woman fawning on her, Molly realized, was a pitiable coward and in terror of the law. And as the older woman's nerves broke Molly took greater courage.

"Perhaps you'll explain the skeleton in the cellar," she said maliciously.

"The skeleton!" gasped the woman falling back against the wall. "The skeleton!"

Molly nodded.

"Somebody has been murdered in this house," she said, and Mrs Barn collapsed.

What should she do? thought the girl. She looked at her watch. It was a quarter past three, and the eastern skies were paling. The woman had gone to her room and lay moaning and weeping upon her bed, and Molly paced her room wondering, wondering.

She did not hear the garden gate open and close, nor Bob Stone's key in the downstairs door. Stone stood for a while in the darkness of the hall, listening. He heard the voluble terror of Mrs Barn and smiled. He heard too the slow pacing of the girl. He crept to the foot of the stairs and listened more intently.

Mrs Barn was weeping, and now and again be caught a disjointed word or two.

"Skeleton…skeleton…"

So the girl had told her! So much the better. Neither woman would go down into the cellar. He himself descended noiselessly, for he had taken off his boots before he had entered the house. He carried a square electric lamp, and this he deposited upon the floor of the cellar. He took little or no notice of the broken brickwork or of the ghastly reminder of tragedy which lay behind. From his hip pockets he pulled two automatic pistols and methodically tested them.

Bob Stone was no lunatic. He was immensely sane. He had been led from crime to crime by his attempt to escape the consequences of his first fall from grace. The tangled web of deception had its counterpart in the automatic fettering of criminality. One crime had begotten another, surely and naturally, and now nothing counted but the great coup which would smother all trace.

He had flung the still-living Frank Weldon into the pool from which the house derived its name. He had hidden his motor-car a mile away from the house in a cleft of the rolling moor, and now there remained Socrates Smith and his brother, a flat-faced woman – and Jetheroe.

Jetheroe would come. Jetheroe who had strangled him until he had written the name of the place to which he had abducted his daughter. Jetheroe would come. That was certain! He extinguished the light and sat down patiently to wait.

Socrates would escape and follow immediately. He would also endeavour to get into touch with the Ashburton police, but all the telephone and telegraph wires to Ashburton came through Exeter and the trunk wires followed the Taunton–Exeter road. Bob Stone had been one of the greatest strategists in the police force in his day. He foresaw contingencies and took precautions. The telegraph system which linked the West of England to London had been his especial study for three or four days, and he had stopped his car in the night to fix climbers to his knees and mount a pole ten miles out of Exeter. There, with a pair of wire cutters, he had worked busily and well. There was further communication between Exeter and the world in the shape of a quadruple line from Salisbury, and he had made a diversion in the night to attend also to that danger. He calculated that it would take six hours to repair the wires, had even considered the possibility of wireless communication between London and Devizes and Devizes and Poldhu, but was satisfied that the time at his disposal was sufficient for his purpose.

He put on the light, took out two large maps, one covered with green and scarlet lines which indicated telegraph communication, and with a fountain pen made neat little marks where he had cut the wires.

The only possibility was that Socrates Smith would stop either at Exeter or at Ashburton to pick up local representatives of the constabulary, but as against this likelihood would be Lexington's eagerness to reach the girl and Socrates' natural desire to come to grips with the man who had killed John Mandle.

He put his maps away and extinguished the light. He would have loved to smoke, but the fumes would have betrayed him.

The girl, sitting by the open window, wondering, hoping, in a panic of fear heard the whirr of a motor-car. Mrs Barn came floundering in.

"He's back, he's back!" she whimpered. And then the garden gate opened and Socrates Smith came running up the path. Molly tore down the stairs to meet him. She was in his arms before Lexington was halfway across the path, and was babbling her incoherent story to Lexington a minute later.

"He's got Frank Weldon!" gasped Socrates. "You don't mean that!"

Rapidly she told all that had happened in the night.

"Do you think Frank was killed?"

She nodded sadly.

"I'm afraid so. He fell like a log," she said and shivered. "Oh, Soc, it is a terrible house, terrible!"

Lexington put his arm round her and squeezed her tight.

"My dear, we're going to take you home straight away," he said.

Socrates was interviewing the woman, but found it difficult to get her story.

She was on the verge of collapse between fear of what would happen and the knowledge that she stood in the presence of one who had the authority of arrest.

"Did Stone say he was coming back?" asked Socrates sharply.

"I don't think he will, but he said so. Oh, that poor young man!" she whined.

"Never mind about the poor young man. You'll have to stand your trial for the part you have played in this felony."

"I'm as innocent as a babe," she almost screamed. "I knew nothing at all about it! He told me that the young lady was mad!"

"You know very well she was not mad, Barn," said Socrates. "This isn't the first time you've been concerned in a case like this, and I rather fancy that you'll go to penal servitude this time."

She flung herself down on her knees before him, a pitiable and an obscene sight.

"I know nothing about it, nothing, nothing!" she wailed. "I didn't know about the skeleton until – "

"The skeleton!" said Socrates. "What do you mean?"

"She found it herself! I never knew anything about it!"

"A skeleton! What are you talking about?" said Socrates.

"She found a skeleton in the cellar," whined the woman, and that was all he could get out of her.

He sought out Molly.

"Don't talk about it," she said with a shiver. "I'm almost fainting with hunger. I've not eaten and I've not slept."

"Well, we'll talk about it afterwards," said Soc gently. "Do you know I suspected a skeleton, but I didn't imagine you'd find it."

He shook the woman into a condition of intelligence, and set her about preparing breakfast. Then, leaving the young people to themselves, he went out through the garden gate and sought for the tracks of Bob Stone's car.

Stone had escaped! He did not doubt that. As to his threat to return, Socrates Smith dismissed that as a piece of deception designed to check his pursuit. He found the track without difficulty. A heavy dew had fallen in the night, and he was familiar with the markings of the tyres of the big limousine.

He followed the track for a quarter of a mile, and then suddenly it turned sharply to the left on to the moor. He saw the broken shrub where the heavy wheels had passed.

Socrates Smith stopped perplexed. Why had Stone taken his car across the moorland when there was a perfectly good cross-road a mile farther on? Possibly he was aware that his tyres would give him away and was trying to baffle pursuit. And yet the direction which the car was taking must bring him to impossible ground. And then a solution offered itself. He was going to dispose of the body of Frank.

Socrates Smith quickened his steps and followed on the track of the wheels. There was no disguising them. In one place they had broken down a bush, in another they had passed through a patch of light soil and had left a deep impression. And now Socrates caught a glimpse of water ahead. This then was the pool. He broke into a run, and then the tracks suddenly disappeared. He searched round and picked them up again. They turned abruptly to the left and apparently headed straight for a patch of stunted bushes.

He pushed his way between the undergrowth and stopped suddenly. There was the car, abandoned. There was no sign of Frank, no sign of Bob Stone. He made a brief examination of the car and found bloodstains upon the Bedford-corded upholstery.

The pool was only a dozen yards away. He pushed through the bushes and came unexpectedly upon a bedraggled young man sitting on the ground, his clothes saturated, and striving to bandage his shoulder with an inadequate pocket handkerchief.

"Frank!" yelled Socrates, and Frank Weldon looked up with a grin.

"Hello, Soc, I heard you coming. Have you got him?"

"He very nearly got you, my boy," said Soc kneeling down by the other's side.

"It's nothing very much. I think the bullet broke my collar-bone. It certainly knocked me out," said Frank. "Have you got him?" he asked again.

"Shut up," said Socrates, busily dressing the long and ugly wound. "Yes, I think he's managed to upset your clavicle. Did he chuck you in the water?"

"He did," said Frank calmly, "but he didn't wait, as I feared, to watch me drown. I could walk ashore, though the bottom of the pool is rather muddy. A very nice man is Mr Robert Stone, and he must have been an ornament to our incorruptible police force."

Frank explained what had happened to him.

"After I fell and lost the use of a good revolver I knew there was no sense in making a fuss," he said. "He picked me up and carried me to his car. The man is as strong as a lion, but he hurt confoundedly. I just lay quiet, hoping that he was going to do exactly what he did, that

175

is, abandon me on the road. I didn't think he'd use the Pool-in-the-Moor – a name which I shall not readily forget," he added. "Did he get away?"

"He's left his car here," said Socrates. "I can't understand it. He wouldn't go on foot."

"He may have another one hidden somewhere. That fellow's a pretty shrewd gentleman," said Frank. "I should imagine that he's planned every detail of this little coup. He hasn't taken Miss Templeton?" he asked quickly.

Socrates shook his head.

He assisted the young man to rise, and they walked slowly back to the road.

"I don't like it," said Frank after a silence. "It isn't natural that he should leave her."

Socrates thought the same.

Yet if the man was in the neighbourhood, what object could he have? Dartmoor was organized for search. The presence of the great convict prison had produced an effective police cordon system which would make his escape impossible.

"Did you see Jetheroe?" he asked suddenly.

Frank shook his head.

"I rather expected he would turn up, but so far he hasn't put in an appearance. Do you think he knows the girl is here?"

Socrates nodded.

"I'm certain he does. That little strangling that went on – oh, you weren't at Prince's Place when it happened," he said, and told the story of Bob Stone's experience. "I knew it was Jetheroe, and I guessed just why he had come into Bob's study and what he wanted to know."

"And yet you shot at the poor devil?"

Socrates grinned.

"I wanted to make him hurry," he said. "I could have killed him twice, and it was against all my better instincts as a revolver-shot to miss him."

They reached the house to find breakfast laid. The girl was overjoyed to see Soc's companion.

"I am afraid I scared you. You saw me at the upper window, but I thought you would recognize me," said Frank.

"You looked awful," said the girl with a smile. "Terrible! I thought you were − a monstrosity that had been living in the house for years and years, and the first time I saw you − "

"The first time?" said Frank in surprise. "Did you see me twice?"

"I saw you passing along the passage when you came into the house," she said, and he stared at her.

"What were you doing? It was the middle of the night."

She made a little face.

"I'm going to tell all about that after breakfast," she said. "I don't want to think about it now."

A distressed and agitated Mrs Barn waited on them through the meal and, despite the gruesome circumstances of the reunion, despite the silent and grisly secret ever present in the girl's mind, it was the merriest meal she could remember. When the woman had been dismissed to the kitchen Socrates told the story of Mandle's murder, a story that was now told for the first time.

THE STORY OF THE MURDER

"I have pieced this jigsaw together," he began, "and I do not think that any of the pieces are missing, except the great base-line of ultimate motive."

"By which you mean?" asked Lexington.

"By which I mean," said Socrates, "the exact nature of the fear which united, and finally divided in such a tragic manner, these two men, John Mandle and Robert Stone. Much of my information I have got from the Record Department at Scotland Yard, but the bulk has been gathered from servants, from Molly here – "

"From me?" said the girl in surprise.

He nodded.

"And from our own observation. When, a little less than a week ago, I received an invitation from John Mandle to spend a weekend in the country and to bring my brother, I was, I confess, considerably surprised. I hadn't seen Mandle for years, and although we were acquaintances, and had met since his retirement, we were not by any means the best of friends.

"During our service together, I had occasion to disapprove of Mandle and his methods. He was a particularly unscrupulous man, and he would go to ends to get a conviction which I think were beyond the limits of honesty and decency. A case in point was the case of Kenneth Ward, or as you know him, Molly, Mr Jetheroe."

"Was he a criminal?" she asked in surprise, and Socrates hesitated.

"He was a man who had got into very bad company," he said diplomatically and truthfully, "and found himself involved in a number of questionable transactions. This was when he was a very young man indeed. Before he could extricate himself he was tried, convicted and sentenced to a short term of imprisonment. When he came out he drifted into the old gang which had brought about his downfall, and helped in the perpetration of a series of frauds which resulted in his arrest by Mandle, and his being sentenced to a long term of imprisonment.

"Mandle worked industriously and for a good reason. In the course of his investigations, he had discovered that Ward was married and had married a very beautiful girl, who was wholly ignorant of her husband's dishonesty. He married her in a fictitious name," said Socrates slowly, "in the name of Templeton."

The girl stared at him.

"Templeton?" she repeated. "It wasn't – it wasn't my mother?"

"It was your mother," said Socrates gravely.

"Then Mr Jetheroe is – "

"Mr Jetheroe is your father," said Socrates; "and remember, Molly, that all his past – is his past. He has suffered for his folly, and I have only recently discovered that his prosperity is not in any way traceable to his earlier misdeeds. I was under the impression that he had put away a lot of money that he had secured by fraud, and that he was living on that now. That is not the case. He inherited a very considerable sum when he came out of prison, from an aunt who was ignorant of his misdeeds. That has been traced beyond question."

The girl was breathing quickly, her shining eyes fixed on Socrates, and it was clear to him that the question of her father's past and his misdeeds was infinitely less important to her than the fact that she had a father living.

"Jetheroe disappeared. He was convicted in another name and dared not write to his wife. Mandle, who had fallen in love with the lady, persuaded her that her husband was dead, and produced certificates to that effect, which undoubtedly he forged. He may have even produced the death certificate. Of that I am not certain. At any rate, he persuaded this poor lady that she was a widow, and married her."

The girl nodded.

"I see now. That is why he hated me – because I was my father's daughter."

"That is probably the explanation," said Socrates Smith. "At any rate, Mandle did his best to send your father back to prison again, and worked day and night to secure evidence of a further fraud and one for which he had not been punished, but should have been wiped out by his earlier imprisonment. Yet he managed to get him a further term of penal servitude.

"Nearly twenty years ago Mandle and Stone decided to leave the force. They were comparatively well-off men, for it is known that they speculated on the Stock Exchange, and that both of them were reprimanded for their association with one or two figures of finance, about whose methods there was some scandal. They seem to have lived together at Hindhead, within a stone's throw of one another, amicably and pleasantly. When Mandle brought his wife and her child to Hindhead they were on visiting terms and remained apparently good friends up to the last.

"But as the years progressed, both men showed some evidence of fear of each other. It was not apparent, perhaps, to the outside world that the man whom Mandle was afraid of was Bob Stone, but it is nevertheless a fact. Seven years ago, Mandle began to put traps on his lawn, fixed electric controls to his doors, and Bob Stone also took precautions. The climax came when Stone professed religion. Now it may not seem to you to mean a great deal or to have any particular significance that Bob was going to address a revival meeting in Godalming, and yet the truth was that that news drove John Mandle into a panic and made him decide upon killing Stone at the first opportunity."

"But why?" asked Lexington in amazement.

"At revival meetings, it is not an unusual thing for a penitent sinner to tell the story of his early indiscretions," said Socrates. "It is a form of religious exaltation very familiar to most psychologists. The penitent finds a peculiar joy in his self-abasement, and it was exactly the possibility of Bob Stone standing up and telling their common secret which so horrified Mandle. Personally I have not the slightest doubt in my mind that Bob Stone had no such intention and that he announced his religious tendency in order to excite just that amount of apprehension in Mandle's mind. I think, too, that Bob Stone knew that the other man was planning his murder, as he undoubtedly was. I received this invitation to visit them and I was surprised, because Mandle isn't the kind of fellow who wants outsiders around and he must have had some particular reason for wanting me in the house.

"I now know that he wanted me there in order to establish an authoritative alibi. My word would carry weight with a jury. If I told them that I had seen Mandle being carried to bed with his legs in such a rheumatic condition that it was impossible for him to walk, no one would suspect him of having hanged Robert Stone."

"Hanged him?" said Frank in surprise. "Was that the scheme?"

Socrates nodded.

"These two men had a system of communicating with one another in moments of emergency. They both understood the Morse code, and it was their practice at a certain hour of the night to look for messages one from the other. Well, to go on. The 3rd of June was the night chosen for the murder, and Mandle laid particular stress upon my being there upon that evening. He asked me to telegraph if I changed my plans, and from what Molly has since told me, he showed signs of irritation that afternoon when I had not arrived by an earlier train, and asked her if a telegram had come.

"For some time before our arrival he had professed to be suffering from rheumatism which made it impossible for him to walk without assistance, and the illness reached its height on the day of our arrival. That was necessary for the purpose of his crime. When Stone came over that afternoon, I guess, rather than know, that he told Stone that his illness was a fake and that he wanted to see him some time that night, but was unable to fix a place because he did not know my plans. That evening Bob Stone was on the watch and received the signal message. The lamp he used was a powerful one and the position of the White House was such that he saw the reflection of the light at one of the windows.

"He was really signalling to Bob Stone. Bob was certain that the hour had struck for his doom, but he could not have realized just what method John Mandle would employ. The rendezvous was the Three Oaks known to them both, and Mandle must have left the house before Molly, for you saw somebody lurking in the bushes."

She nodded.

"That was Mandle," said Socrates. "He waited till you had passed and then he began his preparations. He climbed the tree, lay along the bough immediately over the path. He had with him a rope which he had noosed at the end, and his plan was to drop the rope over Bob's head as he stood waiting beneath the tree, to drag him up by sheer strength, and then, when he had fastened the rope, to slip to the ground and, pulling down the man's hands, handcuff them so that he could not take the weight from his neck."

The girl shuddered.

"We found the handcuffs in his pockets," Socrates went on, "and if you will remember, Lexington, he wore a leather belt about his waist, and I have no doubt that was intended to fasten Stone's feet. It was an ingenious scheme. He could wait by until Bob was dead, remove the handcuffs and the strap and give the death the appearance of suicide. He had already spoken of Bob's religious mania to various people, including Inspector Mallett, and that would explain, to some extent, the tragedy.

"But Bob was on his guard. He came, pistol in hand, ready to shoot. The rope must have dropped and missed him and Bob, looking up, saw the face showing over the bough and fired. Mandle was killed instantaneously and must have lain without a movement or a tremor so that he kept his balance.

"Bob picked up the rope, flung it up into the bough, and then he must have made his escape by the path at the back of the trees. He had then to remove all suspicion from himself and to make it appear that he, also, had been the victim of attack. He did this simply. He tied himself up as a man with a good set of teeth can. Unfortunately for him some of the tow from the rope came off in his teeth. He blew it out – "

"And that was the 'bit of fluff' you found on the pillow!" cried Lexington.

Soc nodded.

"More unfortunate still," he went on, "Jetheroe had seen him, Jetheroe who had come out to look for the man who had frightened Molly. Just as soon as Bob knew that he had been seen, and heard of Jetheroe's search and the story which Gritt told about Jetheroe returning to his house in an agitated state, Bob knew that he must remove Jetheroe from his path.

"I can't understand how he lured him to the Three Oaks, but that is probably susceptible to a simple explanation. The rest of the story you know."

"He must be mad," said the girl in horror.

"I don't think so," answered Socrates quietly. "I think Bob is particularly sane. And remarkably clever. In many ways, I am sorry for him. There is no doubt that he killed Mandle in self-defence, though he would have some difficulty in proving that."

"But the burst of laughter you heard?" said the girl.

"As I said before, that was cleverly and carefully designed," said Socrates. "Bob isn't mad. Bob is a very careful man, so careful that he made a journey to the north of England to buy the goloshes he wore on the night of the murder. By the way, he must have arrived by the main path and the goloshes were intended to throw the police off the track if it came to any kind of trouble."

Frank nodded.

"Incidentally, it enabled him to move noiselessly and was probably a hindrance to him when he was making his way through the bush."

"Well, that's that," said Socrates. "Now, Molly, you're going to tell us all about your skeleton."

She told the story in as few words as possible and she had a startled audience.

"In the cellar, eh?" said Socrates thoughtfully. "Now, I expected to find it in the garden. In fact, I had arranged with a man to cut the grass, for the purpose of seeking the grave!"

Lexington stared at him.

"You expected a skeleton?"

"I expected human remains," said Socrates, and considered it tactful to leave the matter there, for they were in the room where the murder had been committed, as the gaping hole in the ceiling testified mutely to all and the stains on the floor proved beyond doubt.

"You'd better stay here, Molly," he said. "Lex and I will go down and see these unpleasant relics."

"I'll come along too," said Frank, "you'll want a lamp."

The girl rose and, taking off the chimney, lit the smelling lamp.

Soc, with the lamp in his hand, led the way down.

"There are two cellars evidently," he said, looking down, "but the one with the open door is the sepulchre."

They followed him into the cellar. It was empty. Socrates put the light on the ground and knelt by the opening.

"Yes, it's pretty horrible, isn't it?" he said.

He put in his hand and turned the skull and showed a jagged gap.

"That's where the bullet struck, and here," he fingered the dust, "is the residue of quicklime."

He looked round the vaulted room, and picked up an old bag.

"This is a lime bag," he said, "and the bricking-up has been done by somebody who isn't quite used to the work. Now, let me see."

He walked slowly to the lamp and lifted it up, and then before they realized what had happened he had smashed it to the ground!

Lex felt his hand on his arm and was jerked violently backward. Two pencils of flame quivered in the doorway and the explosion deafened them. They could see nothing, for the doorway offered no skyline. Again a shot and this time, Socrates, lying flat on the ground, his arm rigidly extended, sent an answer. Twice he fired and heard a groan and a sound of stumbling feet.

"What is it?" It was Molly's voice at the head of the steps.

"Get away!" roared Socrates. "Into your room and lock the door! Quick!"

He stepped cautiously to the doorway and his caution was justified, for a bullet whizzed so close to his mouth that he felt the wind of it.

Bob Stone, crouching on the stairs, glared down at his enemy in the darkness and fired again, then made a scramble and reached the head of the steps. It was death to follow him, Socrates knew. Presently his halting feet sounded on the stones of the passage and Socrates raced up the steps. He waited for a second, slipped off his coat and gingerly showed the edge of it round the doorway. A bullet struck it with a smack. Bob, halfway up the stairs, commanded the entrance to the cellar.

And now came a diversion.

There was a sound of the front door being opened and it was followed by a further fusillade. Whoever the newcomer was he escaped. Socrates heard the crash of the dining-room door as the stranger leapt to safety, and the staccato rattle of a pistol.

Not a word had been spoken except Socrates' shouted warning to the girl, and he could hear Bob Stone's heavy breathing.

"Ping!"

A bullet flashed past him. Socrates pulled back guessing that the man was now level with the cellar entrance. He jerked out his revolver and fired twice at random and there followed a swift run of feet. The man was on the landing upstairs. Soc came into the hall at the same time as Jetheroe – he had known that the newcomer was Jetheroe.

They said no word. The stairs were deadly to any incautious man who attempted to mount them, for Stone commanded every step from the banisters above.

They heard him smash at the door of the girl's room and his hoarse voice calling, "Come out!"

And then Mrs Barn, who had taken refuge in her own room, opened her door.

"Why don't you go away, sir!" she half shrieked. "Haven't you done enough harm!"

"Go away –" there was a shot and a heavy thud of somebody falling.

Mrs Barn was no longer a possible witness for the prosecution.

"Come out!" roared Bob.

He had one shoulder at the door, his eyes were on the stairs, and the barrel of his pistol rested on the banisters.

The door burst open. There was a shriek. And then Lexington sprang up the stairs three at a time. Twice Bob's gun rapped and then the boy was on him. Down the stairs they rolled, locked together, and then of a sudden Bob Stone went limp.

Socrates jerked his brother to his feet and, pushing him back, bent over the dying man.

Bob opened his eyes and looked round and saw Soc's face. A faint smile twisted his lips. He was trying to say something and Soc lowered his head to listen. The words came faint and jerkily.

And then Soc heard in wonder the man's words. In his delirium he was repeating a charge to the jury, a phantom jury, which he would never face.

"You shall well and truly try – and true deliverance make – in this case before the court – between Our Sovereign Lord the King – and the prisoner at the bar – and a true verdict give – according to the evidence…so help you, God!"

He turned his head wearily and so died.

It was late in the afternoon before Socrates Smith left the house of death. For two sheeted figures lay in the dining-room. The flat-faced Mrs Barn had never known what killed her. Socrates had sent the girl with his brother and Jetheroe to London earlier in the day, and Frank, whose wound was more serious than he had imagined, was at that moment being treated in the Devonshire County Hospital.

Pool-in-the-Moor was in the possession of the Devonshire police and the remains in the cellar had been taken out and were awaiting interment.

Socrates caught the express that left Exeter at five, and at half past nine that night he joined the party in London.

It was a subdued party, but happy nevertheless, for Jetheroe, or Ward, was rejoicing in his new possession, and the girl whom he had watched for so many years with anguished eyes, not daring to tell her that her father was a convicted criminal, was sitting by his side, her hand in his, when Socrates came in.

"No, thanks, I dined on the train," he said when Lex got up and the ancient Septimus, who was really a very old man, had been politely rebuffed in his efforts to supply nourishment to the traveller.

"You came late, Jetheroe."

It was the first reference he had made to the man's appearance at Pool-in-the-Moor, and Jetheroe nodded.

"I had to travel by train, and the trains to Ashburton are very inconvenient," he said. "I did not expect to find you there. Luckily the front door was open."

"How did you manage to get into the garden? That has been puzzling me," said Socrates.

"I climbed the wall," said the other simply. "It was an awful drop for one of my years."

"Well, it is ended," said Socrates with a sigh.

"You seem sorry," said Lexington in wonder, and Soc nodded.

"This has been an interesting case and it has finished so soon. Do you realize that it is only June 10th – only a week, in fact – since we went down to Hindhead? Now, Mr Ward," he smiled at the happy father, "I want you to come across."

"Come across?" said the other, puzzled. "What do you mean?"

"I want that statement of John Mandle's which you took from the cavity beneath the marble chair in his summer house!"

Jetheroe's face cleared.

"I understand," he said. "I wondered what you were referring to."

He put his hand into his breast pocket and pulled out a folded wad of foolscap and handed it to the other.

Socrates glanced at it.

"You left the title page behind, I suppose you know."

"I know now," said Jetheroe.

"Is it of any interest? Does it throw any light upon the Pool-in-the-Moor murder?"

"It was not a murder," said Jetheroe quietly. "That is the extraordinary circumstance. Those two men drifted into crime so

187

naturally that I'm inclined to feel sorry for them," his face darkened, "except for Mandle's wicked treatment of my wife. That I will never forgive," he said in a low voice. "Never!"

"So they drifted to it, did they?" said Socrates. "I wondered how it had happened. Do these people know the contents of this?" he asked; "you haven't read it?"

Jetheroe shook his head.

"I have been too much interested in other matters," he said.

"Is it readable? There's nothing here that would hurt you if it were read aloud?"

Jetheroe shook his head.

"No," he said. "I wish you would read it."

Soc glanced through the pages and looked at the end, raising his eyebrows in surprise.

"Mr Smith – Socrates," said the girl reproachfully, "you mustn't read the end before you begin."

"That is what novel-readers do," Socrates smiled, fixing a pair of pince-nez – she had never seen him wear glasses before – and began to read aloud this remarkable document.

THE SECRET OF POOL-IN-THE-MOOR

I make this statement (the manuscript began) in order that any charges formulated by my late colleague, Robert Stone, may be considered, or examined, in the event of my death from whatever cause. Robert Stone and I entered the police force together and were stationed in the same division. We both made progress in our profession and were eventually transferred to the headquarters of the Criminal Investigation Department.

We were ambitious men, anxious to get on, and neither Stone nor I ever hesitated at any step which secured an arrest and the conviction of an offender. I say this because Stone has frequently said to me in conversation that I was the most unscrupulous officer he had met. This was probably true, and that I did not worry very much about the methods I employed in order to bring an offender to justice. But it is no less true of Bob.

We had not been at Scotland Yard for many years before Bob and I became mixed up with a City crowd of speculators and became involved in certain financial transactions of a shady character. I will do Stone the justice of saying that neither he nor I was aware that we were being let in. We thought that our known characters as officers of the police would prevent swindlers from trying to take advantage of us, but nevertheless, we were robbed in the most barefaced fashion.

The transactions covered a period of twelve months, and we became more and more deeply involved until at the end we found we were about £4,000 or £5,000 on the wrong side of the book. This was a very serious matter for us, for it might mean bankruptcy and our compulsory retirement from the force. The Commissioner of our Department was a very strait-laced man who would not countenance any of his officers being engaged in Stock Market speculations, particularly considering the crowd with which we ran.

We were pressed for settlement and matters looked very hopeless, when a warrant was placed in my hands for execution. It was for the arrest and detention of Emile Deveroux, a cashier of the Lyons Bank, who had absconded with thirty million francs. He was known to be in England and it was believed that he had visited this country before, in order to provide for himself a retreat in the event of his making a getaway. He had planned his robbery remarkably well and had managed to leave France without detection. It was known that he had landed in England and he had been recognized by a customer of the bank in Queen Victoria Street. That was the only clue we had to work upon, that and the evidence of a woman who knew Deveroux and was able to supply us with a photograph.

Bob and I were detailed together to conduct the search for this man and from the first it seemed pretty hopeless. One night Bob and I were dining in a Soho restaurant, talking not about the case, but about our financial position, and hoping against hope that something would turn up that would relieve us of our embarrassment.

In the midst of our talk we saw a man leaving the restaurant.

"That looks like Deveroux," said Bob suddenly jumping up. I hadn't seen the resemblance, but we paid our bill and walked into the street and after a while succeeded in picking up the strange man.

He got into a cab and we followed him but missed him in the traffic. We thought from the direction he was taking that he might be going to Paddington Station, and on the off-chance of that being the case we went straight on to Paddington, arriving just in time to see the West of England express pull out. As it passed us I caught a glimpse of the man we thought was Deveroux in the train. We were in this position, that we weren't sufficiently certain that it was our man to stop the train, as we could have done, or to search at its first stopping place. What we did was to make inquiries at the station. It so happened that there were very few first class passengers, so that we had no difficulty in finding the porter who had handled his baggage.

He had taken a suitcase and a trunk, and the baggage was labelled for Ashburton. Next morning Bob and I went down into Devonshire. We had a pretty free hand, for the Bank of Lyons were willing to spend any amount of money to recover their lost property. It was a bitter cold morning, the morning of the 27th February, 1902, and Bob cursed me that I should have chosen this day for a wild goose chase.

Although the carriages were warmed they were draughty, and it was a miserable journey to Ashburton, which is on a branch line, and a much more miserable journey ahead of us, for we found that a man answering this fellow's description had been seen and had taken a fly to a deserted cottage some miles along the Newton Abbot road. We made inquiries of the local authorities and everything seemed to point to the fact that this was our man. He was a Frenchman, they said. He had bought the property about three years before, and had spent a lot of money enclosing the cottage in a high wall. Apparently he looked forward to the day when he would want a little privacy, although he should have known that by putting up this wall he was drawing attention to his hiding-place.

Evidently the wall had been a nine days' wonder, and Ashburton had forgotten the Frenchman's eccentricity. But the wall presented certain obstacles to us. We could, of course, have got a search warrant, but we did not want to put the local police on the track or to give them any idea that a wanted criminal was in their neighbourhood. It might mean sharing the kudos and whatever reward the Bank of Lyons would certainly give, and also it would result in all sorts of trouble with the local police. So we did not report ourselves to the chief constable, or whatever he is, at Ashburton, restricting our inquiries to the Town Hall and the local estate agents. It was raining and sleeting and a cold north-wester was blowing when Bob and I began our trudge to Pool-in-the Moor.

We would not take a carriage for the same reason, that we did not wish to notify our presence to the local police. It was a long and miserable tramp, and at last we came in sight of this dismal building, standing aloof from the rest of the world, as it seemed, with no other house in sight.

The wall was a very high one. The only door was too thick and heavy to force. There was nothing for it but to scale the wall and, standing on Bob's shoulders, I managed to reach the coping with my fingertips and with an effort to get a grip of the top.

Bob put his hands under my feet and pushed me up, and after a struggle I seated myself on top. We had chosen the wall opposite to that in which the gate was set and I found I was at the back of the house. There was no sign of our man, but smoke was coming out of two of the chimneys. I tried to pull up Bob, but I could not reach far enough down, so I told him to go back to the gate and I would try and open it from the inside.

I crawled along the wall until I came to a little mound on the ground, and then I let myself drop. Apparently I had not been seen, and I made my way cautiously round the house until I came to the gate. Luckily the key was on the inside. I turned it and admitted Bob and we walked straight to the front door. Bob had suggested originally that we should ring whatever bell there was, and pretend we were tradesmen from Ashburton soliciting orders. But there was no bell, and it seemed pretty useless to knock after I had got on to the wall and looked round. To our surprise the front door was ajar, and we walked into the big flagged hall, which was very dark. We heard a clatter of a plate in the room on the right, and throwing open the door I stepped in.

A man was sitting at the end of the table, smoking a cigar, and he put it down slowly on the edge as we made our appearance and half rose. The moment I saw him I knew he was our bird.

"I want you, Deveroux," I said in French, "on a charge of embezzlement and fraud."

I had hardly got the words out of my mouth before there was an explosion. Deveroux fell forward on the table, the blood pouring from a gaping wound in his head. He slid to the floor before we could reach him – dead. And then I saw that the table was covered with packages of thousand franc notes, and an open suitcase lay by his side.

Bob cursed as he jumped forward to snatch the pistol out of the man's hand, for he had seen it before I, and cursed more when he saw he was too late. It is no great credit to a police officer that the man he is arresting has time to shoot himself under his captor's eyes.

"This is a rotten business," grumbled Bob. "Poor devil."

He turned the body over, but Deveroux was stone dead, and then Bob looked at the money on the table, and lifting a packet of bank-notes on to which the blood had flowed, he wiped them on the man's coat.

He looked for a long time at the money and then he looked up and our eyes met.

"John," he said, "there's nearly a million here."

I knew what he meant.

"Nobody knows we've come to Pool-in-the-Moor and nobody will bother to call," he said. "They don't even know that Deveroux is staying here. He may have gone on somewhere else. And, anyway, there'll be no visitors."

I was silent. I could see the tremendous possibilities, but my instinct was all for reporting the occurrence and turning in the money. Bob and I sat down by that bloody table and we talked the matter over and inside out. Then we made a search of the house. The man had very little clothing. His trunk was only half filled. He had slept in the bed upstairs and had apparently cooked his own meal at the kitchen fire. In those days the wall was new, and I think it was the sight of two bags of lime which the workmen had left that put the idea into my head. It was a big risk, we both knew that, but the money was big too. We decided to bury Deveroux and say nothing about his suicide. We thought of the garden, but things buried have a trick of being dug up again, and we looked elsewhere.

Bob suggested the cellars after we had made an inspection of the place, and it was whilst we were looking at the walls that he discovered one of them was hollow and guessed that there was some passageway beyond which had been bricked up. As a matter of fact, it was only a pocket of earth that the builder had been too lazy to fill.

We broke down the wall and we found a space big enough to hide Deveroux. It was a grisly job stripping him, but it was through at last and we covered him with lime and water and worked all through the day bricking up the hole.

Bob was more skilful than I, for my hands were rough and bleeding by the night, but at last the job was done. Deveroux, smothered in quicklime, would disappear, and the only thing to do now was to burn his belongings. All night long we fed the fire in the kitchen. His personal belongings we burnt in the dining-room. Two or three of the banknotes had become bloodstained and those Bob insisted upon putting on the fire. It broke my heart to burn nearly £500, but Bob insisted upon this, and I think he was right. We got together the keys of the place, and we found there were three sets – three for the garden gate and three for the front door. I took one set and Bob took the others.

We packed the money in one of the suitcases and got away the next morning in this manner. Bob started out before daybreak and walked to Newton Abbot, where he hired a buggy and a horse. He drove back by a circuitous route, and I was waiting for him near the gate. As soon as he whistled I knew the coast was clear and went out, locked the door, and we drove to Newton Abbot, where he dropped me at the station with the suitcase.

I went up alone, and Bob returned to Ashburton for the night, leaving in the morning for Cardiff, where I joined him. We agreed to make our records so that it appeared that on the day we were at Ashburton, we were working along the Welsh coast. We went back to town on Sunday and reported our failure, and then had to wait for the affair to blow over. It was Bob who faked the South American story, and who put it about that Deveroux had got clean away. We remained in the force for nearly twelve months before we resigned with a story that we were going on to the Stock Exchange. We had to invent some excuse for our sudden prosperity, and to remove any possible suspicion it was necessary that that prosperity should not be too sudden…

"And that is where the statement ends," said Socrates Smith, taking off his glasses. "There is nothing here about the suspicion he felt toward Bob, or the fear that Bob had of him. Yet it is certain that for years they lived in mutual terror that one would betray the other."

The girl gave a long sigh.

"Now I know what to do," she said. "I was worried about inheriting Mr Mandle's money. Naturally, I can't touch a penny of it."

"I agree," said Socrates Smith quietly. "That money and Bob Stone's estate must be referred to the Lyons Bank. Anyway," he said, "Lex has got quite a lot."

"And so has Lexington's future father-in-law," said Jetheroe.

Lexington's eyes met the girl's.

"Money!" he said contemptuously, and she nodded.

EDGAR WALLACE

BIG FOOT

Footprints and a dead woman bring together Superintendent Minton and the amateur sleuth Mr Cardew. Who is the man in the shrubbery? Who is the singer of the haunting Moorish tune? Why is Hannah Shaw so determined to go to Pawsy, 'a dog lonely place' she had previously detested? Death lurks in the dark and someone must solve the mystery before BIG FOOT strikes again, in a yet more fiendish manner.

BONES IN LONDON

The new Managing Director of Schemes Ltd has an elegant London office and a theatrically dressed assistant – however Bones, as he is better known, is bored. Luckily there is a slump in the shipping market and it is not long before Joe and Fred Pole pay Bones a visit. They are totally unprepared for Bones' unnerving style of doing business, unprepared for his unique style of innocent and endearing mischief.

EDGAR WALLACE

BONES OF THE RIVER

'Taking the little paper from the pigeon's leg, Hamilton saw it was from Sanders and marked URGENT. *Send Bones instantly to Lujamalababa… Arrest and bring to head-quarters the witch doctor.'*

It is a time when the world's most powerful nations are vying for colonial honour, a time of trading steamers and tribal chiefs. In the mysterious African territories administered by Commissioner Sanders, Bones persistently manages to create his own unique style of innocent and endearing mischief.

THE DAFFODIL MYSTERY

When Mr Thomas Lyne, poet, poseur and owner of Lyne's Emporium insults a cashier, Odette Rider, she resigns. Having summoned detective Jack Tarling to investigate another employee, Mr Milburgh, Lyne now changes his plans. Tarling and his Chinese companion refuse to become involved. They pay a visit to Odette's flat. In the hall Tarling meets Sam, convicted felon and protégé of Lyne. Next morning Tarling discovers a body. The hands are crossed on the breast, adorned with a handful of daffodils.

EDGAR WALLACE

THE JOKER

While the millionaire Stratford Harlow is in Princetown, not only does he meet with his lawyer Mr Ellenbury but he gets his first glimpse of the beautiful Aileen Rivers, niece of the actor and convicted felon Arthur Ingle. When Aileen is involved in a car accident on the Thames Embankment, the driver is James Carlton of Scotland Yard. Later that evening Carlton gets a call. It is Aileen. She needs help.

THE SQUARE EMERALD

'Suicide on the left,' says Chief Inspector Coldwell pleasantly, as he and Leslie Maughan stride along the Thames Embankment during a brutally cold night. A gaunt figure is sprawled across the parapet. But Coldwell soon discovers that Peter Dawlish, fresh out of prison for forgery, is not considering suicide but murder. Coldwell suspects Druze as the intended victim. Maughan disagrees. If Druze dies, she says, 'It will be because he does not love children!'

OTHER TITLES BY EDGAR WALLACE AVAILABLE DIRECT
FROM HOUSE OF STRATUS

Quantity		£	$(US)	$(CAN)	€
	THE ADMIRABLE CARFEW	6.99	11.50	15.99	11.50
	THE ANGEL OF TERROR	6.99	11.50	15.99	11.50
	THE AVENGER	6.99	11.50	15.99	11.50
	BARBARA ON HER OWN	6.99	11.50	15.99	11.50
	BIG FOOT	6.99	11.50	15.99	11.50
	THE BLACK ABBOT	6.99	11.50	15.99	11.50
	BONES	6.99	11.50	15.99	11.50
	BONES IN LONDON	6.99	11.50	15.99	11.50
	BONES OF THE RIVER	6.99	11.50	15.99	11.50
	THE CLUE OF THE NEW PIN	6.99	11.50	15.99	11.50
	THE CLUE OF THE SILVER KEY	6.99	11.50	15.99	11.50
	THE CLUE OF THE TWISTED CANDLE	6.99	11.50	15.99	11.50
	THE COAT OF ARMS	6.99	11.50	15.99	11.50
	THE COUNCIL OF JUSTICE	6.99	11.50	15.99	11.50
	THE CRIMSON CIRCLE	6.99	11.50	15.99	11.50
	THE DAFFODIL MYSTERY	6.99	11.50	15.99	11.50
	THE DARK EYES OF LONDON	6.99	11.50	15.99	11.50
	THE DAUGHTERS OF THE NIGHT	6.99	11.50	15.99	11.50
	A DEBT DISCHARGED	6.99	11.50	15.99	11.50
	THE DEVIL MAN	6.99	11.50	15.99	11.50
	THE DOOR WITH SEVEN LOCKS	6.99	11.50	15.99	11.50
	THE DUKE IN THE SUBURBS	6.99	11.50	15.99	11.50
	THE FACE IN THE NIGHT	6.99	11.50	15.99	11.50
	THE FEATHERED SERPENT	6.99	11.50	15.99	11.50
	THE FLYING SQUAD	6.99	11.50	15.99	11.50
	THE FORGER	6.99	11.50	15.99	11.50
	THE FOUR JUST MEN	6.99	11.50	15.99	11.50
	FOUR SQUARE JANE	6.99	11.50	15.99	11.50

ALL HOUSE OF STRATUS BOOKS ARE AVAILABLE FROM GOOD BOOKSHOPS
OR DIRECT FROM THE PUBLISHER:

Internet: www.houseofstratus.com including author interviews, reviews, features.

Email: sales@houseofstratus.com please quote author, title and credit card details.

OTHER TITLES BY EDGAR WALLACE AVAILABLE DIRECT
FROM HOUSE OF STRATUS

Quantity		£	$(US)	$(CAN)	€
	THE FOURTH PLAGUE	6.99	11.50	15.99	11.50
	THE FRIGHTENED LADY	6.99	11.50	15.99	11.50
	GOOD EVANS	6.99	11.50	15.99	11.50
	THE HAND OF POWER	6.99	11.50	15.99	11.50
	THE IRON GRIP	6.99	11.50	15.99	11.50
	THE JOKER	6.99	11.50	15.99	11.50
	THE JUST MEN OF CORDOVA	6.99	11.50	15.99	11.50
	THE KEEPERS OF THE KING'S PEACE	6.99	11.50	15.99	11.50
	THE LAW OF THE FOUR JUST MEN	6.99	11.50	15.99	11.50
	THE LONE HOUSE MYSTERY	6.99	11.50	15.99	11.50
	THE MAN WHO BOUGHT LONDON	6.99	11.50	15.99	11.50
	THE MAN WHO KNEW	6.99	11.50	15.99	11.50
	THE MAN WHO WAS NOBODY	6.99	11.50	15.99	11.50
	THE MIND OF MR J G REEDER	6.99	11.50	15.99	11.50
	MORE EDUCATED EVANS	6.99	11.50	15.99	11.50
	MR J G REEDER RETURNS	6.99	11.50	15.99	11.50
	MR JUSTICE MAXWELL	6.99	11.50	15.99	11.50
	RED ACES	6.99	11.50	15.99	11.50
	ROOM 13	6.99	11.50	15.99	11.50
	SANDERS	6.99	11.50	15.99	11.50
	SANDERS OF THE RIVER	6.99	11.50	15.99	11.50
	THE SINISTER MAN	6.99	11.50	15.99	11.50
	THE SQUARE EMERALD	6.99	11.50	15.99	11.50
	THE THREE JUST MEN	6.99	11.50	15.99	11.50
	THE TRAITOR'S GATE	6.99	11.50	15.99	11.50
	WHEN THE GANGS CAME TO LONDON	6.99	11.50	15.99	11.50
	WHEN THE WORLD STOPPED	6.99	11.50	15.99	11.50

Hotline: UK ONLY: **0800 169 1780**, please quote author, title and credit card details. INTERNATIONAL: **+44 (0) 20 7494 6400**, please quote author, title and credit card details.

Send to: **House of Stratus Sales Department**
24c Old Burlington Street
London
W1X 1RL
UK

Please allow for postage costs charged per order plus an amount per book as set out in the tables below:

	£(Sterling)	$(US)	$(CAN)	€(Euros)
Cost per order				
UK	2.00	3.00	4.50	3.30
Europe	3.00	4.50	6.75	5.00
North America	3.00	4.50	6.75	5.00
Rest of World	3.00	4.50	6.75	5.00
Additional cost per book				
UK	0.50	0.75	1.15	0.85
Europe	1.00	1.50	2.30	1.70
North America	2.00	3.00	4.60	3.40
Rest of World	2.50	3.75	5.75	4.25

PLEASE SEND CHEQUE, POSTAL ORDER (STERLING ONLY), EUROCHEQUE, OR INTERNATIONAL MONEY ORDER (PLEASE CIRCLE METHOD OF PAYMENT YOU WISH TO USE)
MAKE PAYABLE TO: STRATUS HOLDINGS plc

Cost of book(s): —————— Example: 3 x books at £6.99 each: £20.97

Cost of order: —————— Example: £2.00 (Delivery to UK address)

Additional cost per book: —————— Example: 3 x £0.50: £1.50

Order total including postage: —————— Example: £24.47

Please tick currency you wish to use and add total amount of order:

☐ £ (Sterling)   ☐ $ (US)   ☐ $ (CAN)   ☐ € (EUROS)

VISA, MASTERCARD, SWITCH, AMEX, SOLO, JCB:

☐☐☐☐☐☐☐☐☐☐☐☐☐☐☐☐☐☐☐☐☐

Issue number (Switch only):

☐☐☐

Start Date: **Expiry Date:**

☐☐/☐☐   ☐☐/☐☐

Signature: ————————————

NAME: ————————————————————————

ADDRESS: ——————————————————————

——————————————————————

POSTCODE: ——————

Please allow 28 days for delivery.

Prices subject to change without notice.
Please tick box if you do not wish to receive any additional information. ☐

House of Stratus publishes many other titles in this genre; please check our website (**www.houseofstratus.com**) for more details.